# STEALING THE GAME

ALSO BY KAREEM ABDUL-JABBAR
AND RAYMOND OBSTFELD

Streetball Crew Book One: *Sasquatch in the Paint*

# STEALING THE GAME

ALSO BY KAREEM ABDUL-JABBAR
AND RAYMOND OBSTFELD

Streetball Crew Book One: *Sasquatch in the Paint*

# KAREEM ABDUL-JABBAR
## AND RAYMOND OBSTFELD

# STEALING
# THE
# GAME

Ɖɪꜱɴᴇ́ᴩ · HYPERION
LOS ANGELES   NEW YORK

First Edition, February 2015
Printed in the United States of America
1 3 5 7 9 10 8 6 4 2

G475-5664-5-14319

Library of Congress Cataloging-in-Publication Data
Abdul-Jabbar, Kareem, 1947–
  Stealing the game / Kareem Abdul-Jabbar and Raymond Obstfeld.—First
edition.
      pages cm
  Summary: When eighth-grader Chris's older brother, Jax, is caught betting
on the pick-up basketball games that Chris and his friends play, Chris becomes
involved in the police investigation.
  ISBN 978-1-4231-7871-2
[1. Brothers—Fiction. 2. Robbers and outlaws—Fiction. 3. Criminal
investigation—Fiction. 4. Basketball—Fiction. 5. Middle schools—Fiction.
6. Schools—Fiction. 7. African Americans—Fiction. 8. Mystery and detective
stories.] I. Obstfeld, Raymond, 1952– II. Title.
  PZ7.A1589337Ste 2015
  [Fic]—dc23          2013046413

Reinforced binding

Visit www.DisneyBooks.com

SUSTAINABLE FORESTRY INITIATIVE   Certified Sourcing
www.sfiprogram.org
SFI-00993

THIS LABEL APPLIES TO TEXT STOCK

*This book is dedicated to the game*
*and all of us who love it.*
*—K. A-J.*

*To my own Street Crew: Loretta, Max, and Harper.*
*The best team ever.*
*—R. O.*

# BUSTED!

**THE** police officer entered my eighth-grade algebra class, without looking at any of us, and whispered into Ms. Kaiser's ear. She was standing at the whiteboard, her back to the class, halfway through an equation that I didn't understand and probably still wouldn't understand when I took tomorrow's quiz. Ms. Kaiser looked surprised at whatever the officer had said.

Then she turned slowly toward the class and pointed at me.

My heart banged against my ribs and my swollen nose ached even more.

The officer glared at me. He was tall and thin and his uniform looked a little too big, like he'd recently lost a lot of weight. Maybe he hadn't gotten a new uniform yet because he was afraid he'd gain the weight back. Maybe he couldn't afford a new uniform because he was putting his kids through college. I couldn't believe I was even thinking about all that at a time like this.

The officer crooked his finger for me to follow him.

As I stood up, Clay Yothers in the desk behind me whispered excitedly, "Dude, what's the cop want?"

"Is this about what happened to your face?" Simon Zuckerman asked. His eyes were big as softballs. "Is this an arrest?"

I shrugged as if I didn't know.

But I did know.

"He's got pepper spray," Tina Yu said, pointing at the officer's belt full of crime-fighting goodies.

"Forget the pepper spray," Clay said, "he's packing a gun! Dude, what did you *do*?"

Tina was trying to sneak her phone out of her purse so she could take a photo. If she did, it would be posted on Facebook by the time I reached the door. I gave her a sharp look and she slid her hand away from her phone.

Ms. Kaiser looked flustered, her cheeks bright red. She started tugging on her blouse and skirt as if the officer had come in here accusing her of being sloppily dressed. This was only her second year of teaching, and I guess this was the first time she'd had the cops haul one of her students out of class. It was probably the first time this had ever happened at Orangetree Middle School. This was the kind of school with banners for excellence and PTA mothers who planned fund-raisers for new computers and students who belonged to several clubs and teams at once. All the walls were painted in sunshine yellow, I guess to remind us of our bright futures.

As I walked toward the door, I could hear my classmates

whispering, but my blood was pounding so loudly in my ears their words just sounded like boiling water.

When the officer and I left the classroom, Ms. Kaiser's dry marker squeaked against the whiteboard. "Okay, friends, let's examine the variable *y*. . . ."

She'd never called us *friends* before. This whole thing must have shaken Ms. Kaiser, made her think she was back teaching elementary school.

*Friends.* Like we were all best buds. Maybe teachers figured that if they said it enough times, we'd all think it was true. All five hundred of us, linking arms and skipping down Main Street to a Katy Perry song.

"Chris Richards," the officer said with a sour face, like my name tasted bad. "What happened to your face?"

I touched my swollen nose, which was still tender. I knew the purple bruising under my eyes gave me a haunted look.

"Do you know why I'm here?" he said accusingly.

His question made me think of the last thing Ms. Kaiser had said. *Let's examine the variable* y. Only in my head it came out: *Let's examine the variable why.*

Why I'm here.

# FOUR DAYS EARLIER . . .

# "THEY LOOK LIKE CRIMINALS"

**"YOU** guys cheated!" Zach Fallon accused, angrily kicking the basketball off the court.

"Hey, don't kick it," Eric Trebeck said. "You'll break the valve."

"I'm just sick of them cheating!" Zach said.

"We don't have to cheat to beat you," Roger said with a snort. "All we got to do is show up."

Weston, Roger's teammate, chuckled and high-fived him.

"You stacked the teams," Zach persisted. He looked for support from his defeated teammates, Eric and Daniel Hood. "Right, guys?"

Daniel was hunched over, hands on his knees, wheezing like a ball pump, trying to catch his breath.

Eric nodded. "You guys do have all the shooters, Roger."

Daniel, unable to talk while sucking in air, raised a thumbs-up to show he agreed.

Zach added, "And you all play on the school team. We just play here."

*Here* was Palisades Park, the perfectly groomed park

surrounded by perfectly groomed homes. The park had tennis courts, three baseball fields, soccer fields, and a playground covered with a giant orange tarp to keep the sun off the little kiddies. The neighborhoods were so perfect that they attracted families of all nationalities. We had a large Asian population—mostly Vietnamese—and lots of Latinos. On weekends, the soccer field had cricket players from the numerous Indian and Pakistani families in the area.

"Fine." Roger sighed. "Let's mix up the teams. What do you think, Chris?"

I agreed with Zach that Roger had deliberately stacked the teams. We'd crushed them 15–2 in less than ten minutes. It would be even worse if we played them again. Daniel would need an oxygen mask and a team of paramedics on standby.

"I'll swap with Daniel," I said. I walked over and stood next to Zach and Eric.

Zach smiled triumphantly. "Yeah, I'm good with that."

Daniel shrugged and went to stand with Roger and Weston. He was six inches shorter than them and twenty pounds heavier. He looked like half a vending machine. He probably shouldn't even be playing, but his dad had promised him a hundred bucks if he lost ten pounds in six weeks, so here he was.

Roger frowned, clearly unhappy with the decision. "Why don't we just shoot for teams? That's fair."

Of course it wasn't fair. Because Roger, Weston, and

I were the better shooters, the three of us would ~ably end up on the same team again. But Roger didn't care about fair or even having good games. He wanted to win. That was fine when we were playing for the school, but when playing pickup games at Palisades Park, it was ridiculous.

I retrieved the basketball from where it had landed on the grass. When I looked up, I saw two guys in their early twenties sitting on one of the stone benches in the distance, near the snack stand. They were munching on popcorn and drinking blue Icees, staring right at us, like they were in a movie theater and we were the show. I couldn't make out their faces, but one had his short blond hair combed straight up into a fauxhawk. The other wore a black hoodie with the hood up, and dark wraparound sunglasses.

But what struck me was that the guy in the hood had a rolling suitcase standing next to him. Who walks around the park with a suitcase?

"Stranger danger," Weston said, nodding at the two guys. He grinned. "Maybe we should call the cops."

"And tell them what?" Zach asked.

"I dunno. They look like criminals. Who wears a hood when it's eighty degrees out? And what's up with the suitcase?"

"Maybe he's selling stolen iPhones or something," Daniel said.

I handed the ball to Roger. "Your outs."

Usually we'd shoot from the three-point line for possession, but I knew this would stop Roger's complaining about the teams. Instead, he'd take it as a direct challenge.

He grabbed the ball from me with a glare. "Ball in," he growled, and he fired a pass to Weston. Weston quickly spun and banked a five-footer off the backboard.

"I wasn't ready," Zach whined. "I thought we were still talking about those guys."

I couldn't help but look up the slope at the two guys on the bench. Blond Fauxhawk was laughing and throwing popcorn at Hoodie, who seemed to be scowling down at us.

"One to zip," I said. "Let's play ball."

# GAME OVER

**"KA-CHING!"** Weston crowed as he sank another bank shot over Zach's head. He raised two fists high in the air. "Kneel and worship your basketball king, puny mortals!"

"Big deal," Zach said. "Your arms are like a foot longer than mine. You've got ape arms."

"Yeah, but I'm an ape who can score. I'm money, baby!" Weston's nickname on the team was Money Man, because he could hit the bank shot so often. Whenever he scored, someone would yell, "Money Man just made another bank deposit!" Or the short version: "Ka-ching!"

Daniel, who was already breathing hard only five minutes into the game, stood with the ball at the top of the key, panting. "What's—" Deep breath. "What's the score?"

"Ten to four," Roger said, grinning at me. "Guess we didn't need you after all, Chris."

"Guess not," I said.

Even though he was acting like a jerk, Roger wasn't a bad guy. He was big in every way: six feet tall and a hundred and eighty pounds. He wasn't quick on the court—his nickname was Slo-Mo—but there was no one better at setting a pick-and-roll. When players banged into his brick-wall pick, they were dazed just long enough for him to roll toward the basket for the pass. By the time the groggy kid remembered his name and what century it was, Slo-Mo was already steamrolling into his layup. And no one near the basket wanted to take a charge from Roger, no matter how many free throws they got.

"Ball in," Daniel said, and he tossed the ball to Weston. Zach, determined not to be humiliated again (Weston had already hit six bank shots over him), was doing some sort of crazy defense dance that involved jumping around and waving his arms like someone on a desert island trying to flag down a passing ship.

"Are you in training for the rodeo?" Weston joked. "'Cuz you're riding me like I'm a bull."

"It's called defense, dude," Zach said, still jumping and waving. It might have looked weird, but it was effective. Weston tried to find an opening to turn and shoot his bank shot, but Zach was hopping around like he was on a pogo stick.

"Get off me, Zach," Weston said in frustration.

"I'm not touching you," Zach said. I could hear the delight in his voice at knowing he'd rattled Money Man.

Weston passed the ball to Roger, who tried to use his fifty-pound advantage to back me toward the basket. But I'd been guarding Roger in practice for a couple years now, and I knew how to handle him. The secret wasn't in holding my ground. He was too big for that to work. Instead, I'd keep jabbing a hand around him, to swat at the ball. Left, then right, then left, then left again. This scared him, because I'd stolen the ball from him so often before. Usually, he'd just stop dribbling and hug the ball to his chest until he could pass it.

That's what he did now.

Except Zach was still doing jumping jacks all around Weston, making it impossible for Roger to pass the ball to him. And, just as Weston cut around Zach for the pass, I slid between Roger and Weston with my arms up, making it impossible for Roger to pass to Weston. So Roger did exactly what I'd wanted him to do.

He passed to Daniel.

Daniel was surprised, because Roger and Weston had pretty much cut him out of all the plays, just passing to each other and shooting. They let him bring the ball in just to keep him from complaining.

Daniel held the ball, confused about what to do next. So he shot it from the three-point line. The ball fell short of the basket by a foot. I dashed around Roger, snagged the ball out of the air, and fired it to Eric, who was waiting on the three-point line as I'd told him to. Daniel, still stunned by his wild missed shot, finally ran over to guard Eric. But I'd also cut to the three-point line far ahead of Slo-Mo. Eric threw me the ball and I quickly shot the three. The ball rattled against the rim a couple times before dropping through for two points. (Yeah, I know it's weird that we call the shot a *three* when you only get two points, but we like to use the same terms as the pros.)

"Six to ten," I said.

We ran variations of that play two more times, with me shooting the three and scoring twice. That put us tied at tens.

Roger was getting a little tired from my full press on him. And Weston's frustration at Zach's crazy defense made him force a couple of shots that bounced off the backboard and then off the rim.

We were able to take advantage of that lapse for me to score a reverse layup and for Eric to beat Daniel to the hoop for another layup. Then, when Weston left Zach to double-team me so I couldn't take another three-pointer, I bounce-passed to Zach, who sank a baby jumper. The score: 13–10.

Like the good players they were, Roger and Weston adjusted. Roger didn't get flustered anymore when I tried to steal the ball. Weston directed Daniel to just stand in one spot about eight feet to the side of the basket, then used the stationary Daniel as a screen to fire off his bank shot. He did this three times in a row, tying the score.

"Thirteen all," Roger announced loudly, trying to intimidate us. But I could hear the nervousness in his voice. He'd never expected the score to be this close.

In the neighboring court I saw Tad arrive. That's not his real name, just what I call him. It stands for Tiny Asian Dude. Tad was really old and skinny and shuffled when he walked. He neatly folded his jacket and laid it on the grass. He was bald except for a couple scribbles of white hair on top of his head. He wore beige pants and a white shirt with black suspenders. He also wore old man sandals that had more leather than open space, like the ribs of a whale. He carried (he never dribbled) his ancient, beat-up basketball to the free throw line and began shooting.

He was terrible. When I first saw him about a year ago, I thought he was going to be some b-ball Zen master, making every basket blindfolded. Instead, he hardly ever made a basket. And even though he was out here nearly as often as me, he never got any better.

"Hey, Mr. Miyagi!" Weston hollered, and waved.

Roger laughed.

Weston called him that because he looked a little like the teacher in the original *Karate Kid* movie. And also because Weston was the jokester of our team and had to say or do something funny every fifteen minutes or he'd probably faint.

Tad turned, smiled, and waved back.

"C'mon, let's play," I said, before Weston felt the need to say anything else.

Thing is, sometimes I felt like I had more in common with Tad than with these guys I was playing with, a few of whom I'd known most of my life. Tad comes down here every day to shoot baskets. He has to know that the kids who watch him are making fun of him. But he keeps coming and shooting and smiling. He's not thinking about winning, or about playing high school varsity so he can get a scholarship, or anything except tossing the ball toward the hoop. He just loves doing it. That's how I feel most of the time. Or want to, anyway.

"What's the score?" Daniel asked again, standing at the top of the key with the ball.

"Thirteen all," Roger snapped. "If you're not going to make any points, at least remember the score."

"Shut up, Roger," Daniel said. "Me and Zach and Eric were here first. You didn't have to play with us."

Roger started to say something, then stopped. I could tell he knew that he'd pushed Daniel too far and was regretting it. Like I said, Roger wasn't a bad guy, just an intense player.

"Just pass the ball in already," Zach said.

Daniel bounced a lazy pass toward Roger. It was pretty much the same pass he'd made the last four times. Anticipating it, I darted out, intercepted the pass, and cut to the basket. Unfortunately, Roger was waiting for me, his intensity turned up to Volcanic Eruption. He slid his bulk between me and the basket. I tried to dribble around him, but he stayed with me with unusual speed. He wanted to win. More important, he wanted me to lose.

Eric saw my dilemma and ran behind me, Daniel staggering after him. Facing Roger, I bounce-passed the ball backward between my legs to Eric. Using me as a screen, Eric shot the eight-footer for a point, putting us ahead.

Up the slope, I heard Hoodie shout, "Yeah!" and saw

him pump his fist in the air. Fauxhawk slumped angrily. Why did they care so much about our little pickup game? I wondered.

"Fourteen to thirteen," I said, checking the ball to Roger. He tossed it back and immediately got in my face, flapping like a Tasered chicken so I had trouble seeing my teammates.

I faked a pass to the left, then found Eric to the right. He dribbled toward the basket, but Daniel kept with him, determined not to be the cause of the loss. Eric shot the same eight-footer he'd shot before, but this one bounced off the rim. Weston spun inside Zach's defense and tossed an easy layup.

"Fourteens," Roger said. "Next basket wins."

"Win by two," Zach protested.

"Straight up," Roger said.

"We always play win by two," Zach said. "Right, guys?"

"Mostly," Eric said.

"Mostly ain't always," Weston said.

"When did you join the debate team?" Zach said sarcastically.

"Next point wins," I said, and that ended the discussion.

I don't know why kids listen to me. It's not that I'm particularly smart; my grades are mostly B's and C's. And I'm not funny like Weston or clever like Theo, another guy on our school team. I don't threaten or bully like Roger. I don't make fun of other kids and I don't hang with the popular kids at school. In fact, I hardly talk at all. I guess others see my silence as strength, but mostly it's because I'm afraid to say something stupid.

Roger passed the ball to Weston, but Zach was jumping and swatting like he had angry bees in his pants. Weston and Roger kept passing the ball back and forth, trying to get an open shot. They knew if they missed and didn't get the rebound, they might lose.

Finally, too frustrated to wait, Weston forced his way in for a finger roll. But the ball nicked the rim and ricocheted to the side. I was about to grab it when I saw Daniel huffing and puffing toward the ball, his eyes wide with excitement, realizing that this was his chance to do one thing right. I don't why I suddenly thought of Tad, whose missed shots we could hear like the steady patter of rainfall. Whatever the reason, I didn't grab the ball. I let Daniel pick it up. He seemed so surprised to find it in his hands, I thought he might just run off the court with it and be halfway home before he remembered the game.

Weston shouted, "Pass it! Pass it!"

Daniel looked up at the basket, squinting at it as if it were a football field away.

"Dribble in," I said.

He didn't know who said it. Probably thought it was his inner basketball coach. But he did dribble in. Instead of cutting him off and blocking his shot, I stood still and let him go around me. He was right under the basket for an easy layup. He just stood there, staring up.

Zach launched toward him to defend the shot, but I slid into his way, blocking him.

"Dude!" Zach said, trying to squirm around me. I wouldn't let him.

"Shoot!" Roger said. "Shoot, Dan."

And Daniel shot.

# HOT TEMPERS AND COLD ICEES

**ROGER** pulled Daniel into a headlock and twisted his knuckle against Daniel's scalp.

"Ow!" Daniel said, but he was laughing.

"Victory noogie!" Weston announced, pulling Daniel from Roger and delivering his own quick noogie. He released Daniel, who rubbed his head, but had the biggest smile on his face.

"Let's run it back," Zach said. "That was close." He glared at me.

"I gotta go," Weston said. "I haven't finished my algebra homework. If I don't get at least a B on the next quiz, I've got to spend the weekend cleaning the garage."

"I've got a piano lesson," Daniel said, climbing on his bicycle. "Next time, dudes." He waved happily as he rode off.

That was it. Game over.

Zach and Eric also took off, and I could hear Zach grumbling about me as they walked.

Roger sniffed the air and frowned at Weston. "You do smell like an ape, bro."

"Actually," Weston said, "my little sister got a new hamster to replace her dead one and I had to clean the cage this morning."

Weston and Roger picked up their jackets from the grass. Roger turned, looked at me, and smiled. "You're too soft, Chris. Letting Dan have the winning shot."

I didn't say anything.

"See ya tomorrow," Weston said as they walked off together. They lived in the same neighborhood.

In the court next to us, Tad continued to shoot free throws. And continued to miss.

I heard some shouting and looked over at the stone bench where those two twentysomething guys had been sitting. They were on their feet now, hollering at each other. Fauxhawk seemed really upset, repeatedly poking his finger in Hoodie's chest. When Hoodie finally brushed the poking finger away, Fauxhawk threw the remains of his blue Icee in Hoodie's face.

I expected Hoodie to punch him, but he didn't. He just brushed the chunks of blue ice from his face and the front of his hoodie while Fauxhawk yelled a couple more things and then stomped off.

That was entertaining, I thought as I picked up my keys and basketball from the grass. I started walking home, nodding at Tad, who smiled and nodded back. He shot, missed, shuffled after the ball, and carried it back to the free throw line.

"Chris! Hey, Chris!"

I looked around to see who was calling my name.

Hoodie was jogging toward me, his beat-up black suitcase rolling across the grass beside him. When he was only twenty feet away he pulled down his hood and whipped off his sunglasses.

It was my brother, Jax.

# THE RETURN OF GOLDEN BOY

**"YOU** ready to take me on?" Jax asked with a grin. He snatched the ball from under my arm and dribbled onto the court. "Let's go, superstar. Show me what you've got since I've been gone."

I stared at him. He hadn't been home in a year, probably longer. These days our relationship consisted of a Skype call about once a month. The last time he had carried his laptop around his bedroom so I could see what the life of a law student looked like. It looked like every other dorm, but with thicker books.

"You're not scared, are you?" he taunted now. "I'm like a hundred years older than you and haven't played since the last time I was home. Oh yeah, that's when I slaughtered you fifteen to eight."

I dropped my keys on the ground and walked onto the court.

"Man, Chris, you must have grown four inches since last time I was here. You're nearly as tall as me."

"What's going on, Jax? What are you doing here? And who's that guy you were fighting with?"

"We weren't fighting. It was just a friendly disagreement."

"I've met your friends, Jax. I don't know him."

"I've made some new friends. That's allowed, isn't it? Otherwise, I'd still be hanging with Marv Cooley. Remember him? Used to eat his boogers. He came to your eighth birthday party sleepover. I thought Mom was going to throw up your cake when she saw him slurping up a slimy one at the table. Totally worth it to see that look on her face."

I pointed to his suitcase. "What's with the suitcase? You on semester break?"

Jax's face turned serious. "Jeez, Chris, your brother comes home to see you, and instead of a hug, I get the third degree. You join the FBI while I was gone?"

I didn't answer. I didn't know what to say. Yeah, I was glad to see him, but I could tell something was wrong with this picture.

Jax dropped the ball and grabbed me in a tight hug. I hugged back. I'd missed him more than I wanted him to know. I stepped back and said, "You put on some muscle since I last saw you."

"I started lifting weights. It helps relieve the tension of all that studying at my desk. Believe me, bro, law school is just as hard as they tell you it is. It's no joke."

He took a deep breath, as if cleansing himself of those thoughts. "We gonna play, or what?" he said. He smiled a big toothy smile full of bright sunshine and Sunday afternoon picnics and inspirational rock ballads. When he flashed that smile, most people just nodded and did whatever he wanted. That's one of the many reasons he was the Golden Boy.

I picked up the ball. I was no different—I did what he wanted. Not because he expected it. He didn't. He always seemed genuinely surprised and grateful that people went along with him. I did it because I loved and admired him and wanted to be just like him someday. Even though I knew it was impossible.

Mom and Dad wanted me to be just like him too. I'm not sure they realized that, no matter how hard I tried, it would never happen.

So, we played basketball and didn't talk about why he was home or who his crazy friend was or why I kept seeing flashes of fear on his face when he didn't think I was looking.

# HOME IS WHERE THE SECRETS ARE KEPT

**"YOU** did *what*?!" Dad hollered. His face was red and swollen. I couldn't remember the last time I'd seen him this angry. Maybe when I was five and threw up into his open briefcase right before he was due in court. (Turns out orange juice and sardines aren't a great combination for breakfast.)

Mom was just as angry, but she expressed it by standing perfectly still and showing no emotion on her face. If a stranger saw her right then, he'd think someone was giving her a lasagna recipe, not that her son was describing how his life had imploded.

Mom and Dad were both lawyers, and how they were acting now was pretty much how they practiced law. Dad was all passion and pacing and eye bulging and dramatic hand waving. Mom was all cool logic and soothing tones. Dad was hot pizza burning the roof of your mouth; Mom was frozen yogurt cooling your throat.

"You've ruined your life!" Dad announced. "You realize that, don't you? Everything we've all worked so hard for just flushed down the toilet. Why didn't you just throw a bomb through the window and blow us all up? That would have been kinder."

Mom's voice was so low I could barely hear her. "Perhaps you can explain your reasoning, Jax."

"Yes! By all means, Jax!" Dad said, every word turbocharged with sarcasm. "Let's hear your reasoning. I'm sure you have excellent reasons for dropping out of Stanford, one of the most prestigious law schools in the world. A degree from which would have guaranteed you the kind of career most people would kill for."

All eyes were on Jax.

Jax looked over at me. I was sitting on the staircase, out of the line of fire. Mom was standing in front of the leather La-Z-Boy that was referred to as "Dad's chair." Dad was weaving around the family room like a hungry shark, dodging the coffee table, the floor lamp, and Mom as he tried to burn up his energy before he burst into flames.

Jax was sitting on the leather sofa, one arm stretched along the back, one ankle on top of the other knee, looking as relaxed as if he were watching *The Simpsons*. I knew that expression. He would have grinned at me, but he knew that would send Dad rocketing through the roof and into outer space. Stuff didn't affect Jax the way it did normal people. He had some sort of internal off switch that allowed him to always look confident and in control.

I envied that most of all. Which is why I had been so surprised to see those moments of fear at the park.

"Dad," Jax finally said, "you're overreacting. My life isn't ruined."

"Right. I forgot about all those career opportunities at Taco Bell. 'Would you like sauce with that chalupa, sir?'"

"It's just a small road bump. It'll all work itself out." Jax smiled as if he'd already seen the future, when he was sitting in the White House, running the country. "And don't knock the chalupa. They're delicious with hot sauce."

Dad's face turned an even brighter red. "No time for studying, yet you seem to have plenty of time for working out," he said, nodding at Jax's muscular arms. Jax had always been toned and athletic looking, but with his hoodie off I could see how much more muscle he'd put on. "Are you giving up your law career so you can try out for *American Ninja*?"

Jax didn't say anything.

Mom sat down on the edge of Dad's chair. "Just tell us what happened, Jax. Why did you drop out of law school?"

Dad stopped moving and faced Jax, waiting for the answer.

The doorbell rang.

Really? Saved by the bell. Why doesn't that ever happen to me?

Dad took a deep breath and smoothed back his hair, composing himself. "I'll get it," he said to Mom, who'd stood up. I think Dad was relieved to take a break from yelling at Jax. His voice had started to go hoarse.

The three of us remaining didn't say anything. We just stared at the entrance to the living room, waiting for our mystery guest to appear.

We were all surprised to see Dad return with Officer Marcus Rollins, my teammate Theo's dad. He was dressed in his Tustin PD uniform, with his big black belt sagging under the weight of a gun, handcuffs, pepper spray, and a few things I didn't recognize.

He nodded at me. "Hey, Chris."

I nodded back. "Hey, Mr. Rollins."

"Marcus," Mom said with a big smile, giving him a hug. "Is this about the mutilated bodies I've been burying in the backyard?" Mom had a weird sense of humor, which she only used with her close friends. Over the years, she and Mr. Rollins had tried to get Theo and me to do stuff together, but his friends were all brainiacs and mine were jocks, so neither of us was interested. Now that Theo was on the school basketball team, we'd gotten used to each other.

Officer Rollins chuckled. His manner and expression told me this wasn't a serious visit.

"No. It's the department's policy to let the first six dead bodies slide. But if there's a seventh, I might have to write you a ticket."

"You guys are so morbid," Dad said with a laugh, as

if we'd all been sitting around playing a spirited game of Monopoly. "Marcus, you remember Jax?"

Jax walked over and shook Officer Rollins's hand. It was weird to see my six-foot-one brother look up to an even taller guy.

"Good to see you again, Officer Rollins," Jax said.

"I guess a fancy Stanford law student can call me Marcus," Officer Rollins said.

I waited to see who would burst a blood vessel first, Mom or Dad. But both nodded happily as if Jax were still at Stanford and the world was a big, shiny golden apple.

"Hard to believe it's the same Jax I used to carry on my shoulders." Officer Rollins ran his hand over his bald scalp, his black skin glistening from the recessed lighting over his head. "Back then I had the most glorious Afro. And a big ol' mustache." He traced above his lip, as if he expected to find the mustache there, like he'd misplaced it for all these years. "I looked like Shaft."

"Shaft was bald," I said, remembering the movie I'd seen over at Roger's house.

"Not the Samuel Jackson Shaft," Officer Rollins said with a frown. "I'm talking about the original. Richard Roundtree." He said the name with awe, like a priest might say the pope's name.

"Can you dig it?" Dad said in a weird hipster way, and the two of them laughed. Clearly this was some sort of old folks' reference that I didn't get.

"Wasn't the one with Samuel Jackson R-rated?" Mom

suddenly said, turning toward me like this was a cross-examination.

Really, Mom? Is now the time to have this discussion again? I'd been watching R-rated movies since I'd turned twelve. In fact, Dad took me to see a horror film that was rated R. Oddly, Mom was okay with me seeing an R-rated movie if it had violence and language. But if it was R because of sexual content or nudity, she didn't want me to go. Naked people, no. Hacked-up people, okay.

"Anyway," Officer Rollins said with a tired sigh, "the department's been going door-to-door to warn people about the rash of burglaries we've had around here lately."

"Right," Mom said. "We got an automated phone call."

"Apparently, that wasn't effective enough. We've had three more since the calls."

I'd heard something about it at school. The crooks were breaking into garages and taking all they could carry.

"How are they getting into the garages?" Dad asked. "They're all on coded remotes."

"We don't know yet," Theo's dad said. "They've hit a dozen homes in the area in the last three months."

"By 'area' do you mean *this* neighborhood?" Mom asked.

"Not yet. But the last house was only a few blocks away, on Champion."

Mom looked at Dad. "That's pretty close."

"Who do they think it is?" Dad asked. "Kids, or professionals?"

Officer Rollins shrugged. "It's a pretty smooth operation

for kids. They've made off with hundreds of thousands of dollars' worth of property. Somebody's going to do some serious jail time, kid or not."

Why was he looking at me?

He continued, "So, just be on the lookout for anything suspicious. People you don't know driving around. You see anything, give us a call and we'll check it out."

Mom and Dad walked Officer Rollins to the front door.

When they were out of the room, Jax said, "Man, I go away and the place turns into a crime zone. Pretty soon we'll have gangbangers spray-painting the mailboxes and Mafia hit men patrolling in Best Buy."

I smiled. I missed his sarcasm.

Then Mom and Dad reappeared and Dad said, "Let's get back to why you dropped out of Stanford after everything your mom and I did to get you there."

Jax took a deep breath, like he was about to dive to recover something from the bottom of the ocean. "I didn't exactly drop out," he said quietly. "I'm on academic leave. It was either that or flunk out."

"*Flunk out?!*" Dad wailed. "Flunk out!" He was moving again, hands chopping the air like he was fighting off a gang of attacking ninjas.

I'll save you from the rest of the argument. I tiptoed up the stairs while Dad continued to rant and Mom cross-examined. Then Jax got mad and *he* started to rant. Then even Mom was ranting at both of them to stop ranting.

Rant. Rinse. Repeat.

I closed the door to my room and flopped onto my bed. My backpack was still where I'd tossed it earlier, before I had taken off to play some basketball. It held the homework I had to finish. Algebra, Spanish, and social science.

But instead of hitting the books, I hopped off my bed, opened my bottom desk drawer, and removed the false bottom I'd made last summer, when my parents were busy moving their law office to a bigger location. I pulled out the papers I kept hidden there and put them on my desk.

Like I said, home is where the secrets are kept. And this was my big secret.

One of them, anyway.

# MY 3 DARK SECRETS

**HERE'S** Dark Secret No. 1: I like to steal.

Yeah, I know it's wrong, so don't give me The Lecture about how stealing is a crime and morally wrong and would I want someone to steal my computer and blah, blah, blah.

When the guidance counselor at school asks me what I want to be when I grow up, I always say something like *lawyer* or *businessman* or something else she wants to hear. But in my head I'm thinking *master criminal*.

Before you pull out your cell phone and 911 on me, here's Dark Secret No. 2: I've never stolen anything. Not a pack of gum, a pencil, not even the dollar bill I found in Spanish class last week. I gave it to the teacher, who asked the class if anyone had dropped it. Five hands shot up.

Anyway, I don't want to be a petty thief. I see myself all dressed in black, dropping through some rich guy's skylight, dodging infrared alarm beams, and finally grabbing some art masterpiece worth millions that he'd bought with money made dishonestly. I'd be like Robin Hood— except I'd keep some of the money so I could have a cool beach house with skylights. I'd give the rest to Greenpeace, because they're trying to save whales.

Dark Secret No. 3: I draw comic books.

This is the darkest secret of all, because if my parents found out, they would probably throw a fit worse than the one they were throwing right now with Jax. My cell phone would be taken away. My computer use would be restricted to homework only. Bars on the windows were a possibility. Electrified fences and toothy Rottweilers might be involved.

Here's why: I'm supposed to follow in Jax's footsteps.

And, despite what you saw today, those are really big footsteps.

Jax has always been the family's Golden Boy. He was the star pitcher of his Little League team, which started a domination of all sports—one that continued throughout high school and college. Star football quarterback. Star basketball forward. Star volleyball setter. Tennis, golf, water polo. Whatever sport, Jax excelled. More important, unlike a lot of his teammates, he was never a jerk about it. He didn't show off, brag, or hog the ball. In basketball he was known for passing as much as shooting. He went out of his way to make his teammates look good. Obviously, everyone loved him.

If only sports had been his sole area of accomplishment. No such luck.

He was also a straight-A student, the prized pupil of every teacher. His essays won contests, his test scores broke records, his scholarship offers in both sports and academics made guidance counselors weep with joy. I had hoped that our nine years' age difference would prevent any comparisons. Nope! In almost every class, when I walked in for the first time, the teacher would ask if Jax was my brother. They always asked with a big dopey grin, looking so hopeful that I hated to say yes, because I knew how disappointed they were going to be. There would be no weeping for joy because of me.

The only thing I had in common with Jax was basketball. It was the only thing I did well, maybe as good as he did.

That and my comic books.

# GOLDEN BOY VS. BRONZE BOY

**MY** parents don't know I read comic books, let alone write and draw them. It's not that they have anything against comics—Dad used to read them as a kid, and he was the one who took me to the comic book store when I was around eight to give me a tour of his childhood favorites: Flash, Superman, and Green Arrow. Jax never was into them, which made them even more appealing to me. It was something just between Dad and me.

Here's the thing, though: I think my parents figured that comics were a gateway into reading, and that once I was able to read "real books," I'd pack away childish comics along with LEGOs and Barney the purple dinosaur.

Except I didn't.

And the reason I don't want Mom and Dad knowing about my reading or drawing comics is that one of two things would happen: (1) They'd have something to use to punish me, like taking them away if I wasn't doing something they wanted (which they did with TV, movies, Xbox, and my computer). Or (2) They would make me take art lessons to encourage me to become the best graphic novelist of all time, asking me daily about my progress, wanting to read every word I wrote, examine every drawing I made. It's basically why I stopped playing the guitar.

Comics are my thing now—as long as they never find out about it.

They are not part of the Richards Family Master Plan. The RFMP is for me to do everything Jax has done, but better. Clearly, the RFMP is not working.

Like Jax, I'm good at most sports. Throw a ball into the air in the middle of a crowd and I'll be the first to grab it. I like playing, and even though I never say it aloud, I like being on a team. There's something cool about a bunch of guys from different families and cultures and backgrounds all working together toward one goal. I know most people think that goal is winning, but I don't think it is. I think the goal is just to be on a team. Winning is the by-product, the same way Jell-O is made from gelatin, a by-product of boiling animal bones, connective tissues, and intestines. Mostly, winning gives us something to talk about, our own language that makes us feel special.

I need that feeling of being special, because whenever I'm compared to Jax, I don't feel even close to special.

Unlike Jax, I suck at school. I'm not a complete dummy. I get A's in English. I really like reading the stories and poems, and even though I don't say it aloud (see my pattern?), I actually understand most of the hidden meanings and stuff that Mr. Laubaugh brings up and that make everyone else groan. A couple weeks ago we read "The

Tell-Tale Heart" by Edgar Allan Poe, and I liked it so much that I went online and read a bunch of his other stories. Poe was one creepy dude. Of course, I'd never mention any of this in class, or everyone would think I'm kissing up to the teacher. So the Legend of Quiet Chris continues.

*"Are you insane?!"* my father yelled so loud that it actually rattled my door. "That's not a rhetorical question, Jax! I truly want to know if you've been examined by a psychiatrist!"

I heard Jax laugh. Which caused my dad to yell even louder.

I'm also good at history. There's something comforting about history. Like sometimes I think about some boy my age a hundred years ago, or two hundred years ago, or a thousand years ago, and I know they were probably sitting at their desk or by the river or in a stable and doing something their parents didn't want them to do.

It's math and science that are killing me. I hate math and have no interest in it, so I'm just treading water there, trying not to fail. But I actually like science and learning how birds fly and why we have volcanoes and where Jell-O comes from. It's just that there are so many technical terms to memorize for the tests that I get them mixed up. And, no, I'm not dyslexic. My parents had me tested. Twice.

I think they would have been relieved if I was dyslexic, because that would explain my math and science test grades. And they would have been able to formulate a plan of action (they loved to come up with plans of action) that would have included more testing, medication, tutors, and therapists. Unfortunately for them, I'm just bad at those subjects.

Also unlike Jax, I'm not good at social stuff. Jax could walk into a prison filled with the worst, most ruthless, most violent men in the world and he'd come out with three close friends. And at least one of the guys would be offering to set him up with his sister. When Jax was in high school, if someone was invited to a party, the next question was, "Is Jax going to be there?" And, to tell the truth, everything was a lot more fun when Jax was there. He was funny and lively and daring and kind. Even though he was nine years older than me, he was always taking me along with him and his friends when they went to the beach or the movies or Disneyland. He didn't have to, he just did. And he always made me feel like I was part of the gang, not just some punk kid brother he had to drag along.

See? You wish you knew him, too, don't you?

To my parents, Jax was the Golden Boy, who shined like the sun. I was more the Bronze Boy. Bronze looks like gold from a distance, but when you get closer you realize it's not as attractive, not worth much, and is easily forgotten.

# MY FAMILY'S NO. 1 DARK SECRET
## (P.S. DON'T TELL ANYONE! SERIOUSLY!)

**NOW** I'm going to tell you something I probably shouldn't. Something the family rarely talks about. And then only in a hushed voice, like kids planning a party they don't want their parents to know about.

I was a "designer baby."

No, it was nothing to do with fancy diapers or silver spoons or an English nanny.

The other term for me is "savior sibling."

What it means is that I wasn't conceived in the usual way that they tell you about in health class or romantic comedies. And my parents didn't decide to have me because they were overwhelmed with a desire for another child. They had their hands full with the one they had.

They decided to have me to save Jax's life.

I'm not going to go into the medical specifics, but he had a blood disease that required having transfusions every three weeks and a bunch of painful injections that took twelve hours to complete. The doctors didn't give him much hope of living to his tenth birthday.

The only thing that *maybe* would save him—and it was

a very, very shaky maybe—was a transplant of blood cells with the same immune system genes. For that, they would have to make another baby. There were a billion things that could go wrong, the most probable one being that I wouldn't be a match. But my parents decided to take the risk and have me. They used stem cells from my umbilical cord to jump-start Jax's immune system, and then blood from my cute baby self to keep him going. For most patients in Jax's position, recovery is slow and tedious and even then not necessarily guaranteed. But Jax defied all medical expectations by making a full recovery. I think the whole experience is what drove him to excel in both athletics and academics. Like he was proving to everyone that they had made the right decision going through all that pain for him.

Like I said, we rarely talk about it. Not because we're ashamed or broke any laws, but because there are a lot of nut jobs out there with all kinds of opinions about everything, especially what's moral and what's not when it comes to science. I've read about other families that have done the same thing and received death threats from their neighbors. So you can see why we don't broadcast the whole "savior sibling" thing.

Except sometimes Jax jokingly called me SP (for Spare Parts). He told me once that English royalty used to refer to their children as "an heir and a spare." That meant they would have one child who was expected to inherit the throne, then another "spare" child in case something happened to the heir. When he called me SP, I'd call him BB, for Blood Bank, since I made so many deposits of my blood into him. That was our private joke.

He doesn't go around thanking me all the time for saving his life. After all, I didn't really choose to do it. But there is a special bond between us because of what happened.

Or so I thought.

Now I wasn't so sure what was going on with him. And it scared me.

# ? SAVES THE WORLD

**I WAS** sketching a new supervillain when my bedroom door suddenly flew open.

In a panic, I plunked my laptop on top of my sketches and began to type furiously. My heart beat as rapidly as my fingers clacked on the keyboard.

"Relax, Stan Lee," Jax said with a chuckle. "I'm not here to bust you."

I stopped typing and waited for my blood pressure to go down. Fear of discovery had left a weird taste in my mouth, like I'd been sucking on a rusty nail. "Thanks for the heart attack, Jax," I said.

"Don't say I never gave you anything, SP," he said.

"Ditto, BB," I said.

He closed the door behind him and leaned against it, releasing a deep sigh and pretending to wipe his brow. "Whew!" He grinned. "And that was only Round One. Can't wait to see what Mommy and Daddy dearest have in store for me tomorrow, after they've had all night to discuss it." He made the sound of an explosion while his hands pantomimed an expanding mushroom cloud.

"You can't really blame them," I said sternly. I was instantly annoyed with myself for taking Mom and Dad's side. But I was mad at Jax for not telling me he'd dropped out of Stanford, a place I had no hope of ever getting into. Or that he was coming back home. I get his not telling Mom and Dad, but I'm his *brother*! "You did kinda spring this whole dropping-out-of-law-school thing on them."

"It's like a Band-Aid, bro. Just yank it off before you have time to think about it. Less painful that way."

I stared at him, trying to figure out why he was acting so weird. He wasn't usually this sarcastic about Mom and Dad.

He walked over to my desk and pulled the sketches out from under the laptop. "Who's this?" he said, holding up the supervillain I'd been working on.

Remember earlier when I said I drew comics? I may have exaggerated my ability. My characters look stiff and mechanical, like they were drawn by a circus dog with a pencil in his mouth. Basically, I draw a vaguely humanoid shape, then I design the costume and describe the powers with arrows pointing to appropriate body parts. Thinking up powers is what I'm good at. I'm hoping that someday I'll meet a real artist who might want to work with me. At school, I'm always secretly looking at kids' doodles, trying to find someone who can actually draw.

"Where's Master Thief?" he said, referring to my main superhero. Master Thief is the me I was telling you about earlier: the sophisticated thief who can go wherever he wants because he can break into anything. No secrets are safe from him, and he can't be contained. You could lock him in a steel box and drop it into the ocean and he'd find a way out. I'm still not sure what superpowers to give him. I could give him super-hearing so he can hear the tumblers in safes that he's cracking. Or super-vision so he can see all the traps that are laid out to capture him. But I don't want to make it too easy for him. There has to be risk, or the story will be boring. It's like Superman, right? He's got dozens of superpowers so it's hard to believe anyone in the universe can defeat him.

"These are the villains Master Thief has to fight. I figure if I get them right then I'll know what powers Master Thief needs."

"If he's a thief, why would he fight villains? Isn't *he* a villain?"

"Well, he's a villain to some, just like Catwoman and Black Canary are, but he also fights against really bad guys."

"Sounds like an identity crisis."

"He's complicated," I said sharply, hoping to end the conversation. Truth was, I hadn't really figured it all out yet.

He nodded as he leafed through my sketches. He held up the sketch of a man with six arms, each one holding a different weapon. "Who's this?"

"I call him Armed and Dangerous."

Jax laughed. "That's funny, Chris. Really funny. Did you mean it to be funny?"

I shrugged. I had meant it to be funny, but for some reason I didn't want to admit it.

He mussed up my hair. "You're a funny guy. Who knew?"

No one had ever called me funny before. Sometimes when kids were joking around at lunch or in the locker room I would think of something funny to say, but I never actually said it. I think because by now everyone expected me to be the strong and silent jock. If I suddenly started joking around and acting all goofy, they might lose respect for me. Sometimes I wasn't sure which was worse, losing their respect, or keeping it and not being able to do things I wanted to do.

"I thought you were going to change Master Thief's name," Jax said, sitting on the edge of my bed.

"Yeah, I am. I just can't think what it should be."

"I like Master Thief."

I shook my head. "Too normal. Doesn't suggest any kind of powers. I can't name him until I figure out what his powers are."

"What about Ultra Thief, or Super Taker? Oh, I've got it: That's Mine."

I laughed. "That's Mine?"

"Okay, man, you're the artist. I don't want to interfere with creative genius." He flopped back on my bed and let out a long sigh. "Man, I am beat. Getting yelled at is exhausting. Nice to know Dad hasn't lost any volume in his old age."

I didn't say anything. Something didn't feel right about this whole situation. Not about him dropping out. Or coming home. Or that guy he was with in the park who threw his Icee on him.

"What really happened, Jax?"

"What do you mean?"

"Why'd you drop out of law school?"

"I told you, Chris, I didn't drop out. I just took a leave of absence. That's a real thing. I've got official paperwork to prove it."

I made a face. "You've never failed at anything before. Not even close. I can't believe this was too hard for you."

He closed his eyes and crossed his hands over his chest so that he looked like a corpse. "Here lies the body of Jackson Peter Richards. He finally failed at something and it killed him."

"Stop acting like a jerk," I said, feeling the anger boiling up in me. "I'm not Mom or Dad."

He opened his eyes and sat up. He looked at me for a minute, then smiled sadly. "It's not easy being the Golden Boy, Chris. Everybody expects you to win. Always." He shook his head, as if trying to shake the memory out of his mind. "This time I didn't win. I don't know why. The courses were hard, but not that hard. The students were competitive, but basically nice. The teachers were helpful. I wasn't distracted with sports or girls or drugs or any of the usual excuses. And yet . . ." He shrugged. "And yet, I didn't seem to care."

"There's got to be a reason why," I insisted. "There's a reason for everything."

"You sound like Mom and Dad."

"That doesn't mean I'm wrong."

He laughed. "There's no mystery to solve, Chris. Big brother screwed up, and now I'm going to crash at home for a couple months while I figure things out. If I were you, I'd quit worrying about me and start preparing yourself."

"Preparing myself for what?"

"Now that I'm the Bad Son, you've been promoted to the Good Son. Which means Mom and Dad will be pushing you even harder."

I knew he was probably right. Which meant my only hope was to return him to the status of the Good Son, the Golden Boy.

"You going back to Stanford?" I asked hopefully.

He shrugged again. "It's an option. Among others."

"What other options? What else can you do if you don't finish law school?"

"Butcher, baker, candlestick maker." He flexed his huge bicep. "Enforcer for the Mob."

"I'm serious, dude."

He nudged my leg with his foot and sang in a Jamaican accent, "'Don't worry, be happy.'"

I knew he was just trying to end the conversation. "I'm not the same kid I was when you left for law school, Jax. You can tell me things."

Jax's face turned serious and sad. "I know, bro. I know.

It's just that there's really nothing to tell. No sob story. No excuse. I just failed."

I knew he was lying. I always knew with him. Not that he couldn't tell whopping lies and get people to believe him. If I overheard him lying to someone else, I'd believe him, too. But he could never lie directly to me without me knowing. That didn't stop him from trying, though.

"Who was that guy in the park? The one who threw the Icee on you?"

"Just a guy I know. No one important." He looked away, avoiding my eyes.

I decided not to push him. He wasn't going to tell me anyway. Not yet. But there definitely was something mysterious going on with him, and I was going to find out what it was.

But I would need help. And I knew just where to find it.

# THREE DAYS EARLIER . . .

# RIDDLE ME THIS

**"OKAY,** students, here is today's brain-busting riddle." The class quieted as Mr. Laubaugh sat on the edge of his desk and faced them. He liked to begin each English class with a riddle to, as he put it, "kick-start our brains."

"What's the prize?" Clancy Timmons asked from the back row, where such questions always seemed to come from.

"Prize?" Mr. Laubaugh said, pretending to be shocked by the question. "Why do you need a prize? Isn't knowledge enough of a prize? Or the respect of your peers for having solved a tough puzzle?"

The entire class shouted, "No!"

He laughed and said, "Message received." He picked up a DVD from his desk and held it up for all of us to see. "The prize is this copy of the beloved classic John Hughes film *Pretty in Pink*, starring the incomparably quirky Molly Ringwald."

"Molly Ring*worm*?" Clancy said and snickered.

"Ah, Mr. Timmons," Mr. Laubaugh said, "I can always count on you to find the humor in everyone's name. We all fondly remember how you were able to turn substitute teacher Mr. Farley into Mr. Fartlips."

"One of my better ones," Clancy agreed.

"A rare talent indeed," Mr. Laubaugh said.

If it were any other teacher, I'd think that he was making fun of Clancy. But Mr. Laubaugh didn't make fun of students, no matter what stupid thing they did or how much they deserved it. He treated everyone with cheerful respect and the students liked him for that.

"What's the riddle?" Brooke Hill said impatiently. She was the richest girl in school—and the prettiest. But she was also the most competitive person I had ever known, and I've played every kind of sport since I was five. As another student once said of her, "She'd rather gnaw off your leg than let you beat her in a race."

"Let's hear it, Mr. Laubaugh," Theo said. Theo, one of the few African-American students in the school, was six-foot-four after a six-inch growth spurt last summer. That made him taller than his dad, Officer Rollins, who'd been to our house the night before to warn us about the garage burglaries. Right after his growth spurt, Coach Mandrake had talked Theo into joining the basketball team, even though he'd never played. He was skinny and awkward and clumsy. After a rough start, he was finally starting to fit in with the rest of the team. Not that he needed to. He was also one of the smartest kids in the school, once on the Brain Train team of eggheads that challenged other schools to see who was the brainiest.

He was the person I really needed to talk to today.

Mr. Laubaugh cleared his throat dramatically. "Okay, here we go. What gets wetter and wetter the more it dries?"

While I was still repeating the riddle in my head, two people called out.

"A towel," Theo and Brooke said at the same time.

"You've heard it before?" Mr. Laubaugh asked.

"No," they both said, again at the same time.

Brooke glared at Theo with a leg-gnawing expression.

Someone in the back fake-coughed. "Nerds."

"Let's try a harder one," Mr. Laubaugh said. "The man who invented it doesn't want it. The man who bought it doesn't need it. The man who needs it doesn't know it. What is it?"

Silence.

Brooke closed her eyes and scrunched up her nose. I knew she was a handful, but I couldn't help thinking how cute she looked like that. She reminded me of Lucy in the Peanuts comics.

"Give us a hint," Dave Jaspers said.

"No hints," Mr. Laubaugh said. "Just keep your eyes on the prize. This special edition DVD from my home collection. Played on the very night I asked Mrs. Laubaugh to marry me, so we know it has magical powers." The prize was always a DVD from his home collection, because he was downloading all his movies onto a hard drive and getting rid of his DVDs, which numbered in the thousands.

"What did she say?" Clancy asked.

"He called her Mrs. Laubaugh, doofus," Brooke said. "That should be a clue."

Clancy whispered something to Jeremy in the desk next to him. They both chuckled.

"Give up?" Mr. Laubaugh asked the class.

"Yes," most of the class chorused.

"No!" Brooke snapped.

"Can you repeat it?" Dave Jaspers said.

Everyone groaned.

Brooke glared at Dave and repeated the riddle word for word: "The man who invented it doesn't want it. The man who bought it doesn't need it. The man who needs it doesn't know it. What is it?"

I had no clue what the answer was. I never did with these riddles. But I still liked them and admired people who could figure them out, which was almost always Theo or Brooke.

"Bzzzzzz!" Mr. Laubaugh said. "Time's up."

"Wait—" Brooke protested.

"It's a coffin," Mr. Laubaugh said. "The man who invented it doesn't want it, because that would mean he'd be dead. The man who bought it doesn't need it, because he's not dead yet. The man who needs it doesn't know it, because he's already dead."

Brooke snorted. "You have to give us enough time."

Clancy said from the back, "That's pretty dark, Mr. L. Are you sure you're allowed to talk to us about death and such?"

Mr. Laubaugh smiled as he walked over to the whiteboard. He wore baggy pants and a maroon sweatshirt with some sort of stain near the collar. Egg, I thought. He wore baggy pants and sweatshirts every day, and every day there was some sort of food stain somewhere.

"We talk about everything in this class," he said. "Especially while we're reading *The Catcher in the Rye*." He then wrote on the board: *Who is good? Who is bad? Why?*

During class discussions I didn't raise my hand unless a lot of other kids did, to decrease the chances of my being called on. That strategy usually worked. It's not that I didn't know the answers. I did in this case, and I was actually excited to hear the discussion, because I loved the book. But whenever I did get called on, what I said never seemed to be what I meant to say. It was like one of those voice changers you can use to make yourself sound like a robot or Darth Vader, only this changed my actual *words*, so I sounded like Lame-o McLameson.

My motto was something that, according to Mr. Laubaugh, Mark Twain had said: "It's better to remain silent and be thought a fool than to speak out and remove all doubt."

When the class was over and we were all funneling out the door, I grabbed Theo by the elbow, pulled him to the lockers, and said quietly, "I need your help."

He looked startled, like I'd said, "I just ate your dog." Probably because I'd never asked anyone for help before.

"You mind?" Brooke said, shoving past us. "If you boys

want to discuss the best place to inject steroids, please do it elsewhere. Some of us have to get to class."

Theo frowned at her, but I grinned. I might have been the only student in the school who thought she was funny. But then, my brother was the only person in the world who thought *I* was funny. So we had something in common.

"What's up, Chris?" Theo asked as we walked through the crowded hallway.

"I need a detective," I said. "And you're the closest thing to it that I know."

A smile stretched across his face. "I'm in!"

# THE BULLDOG MYSTERY

**"BRICK** is innocent!" Sharon Currie yelled so loudly that I covered my ears.

"Brick is guilty!" Damon Currie yelled right back at her. "And you're gonna pay for a new iPhone."

"I'm not paying for anything!" Sharon yelled again. "Because Brick didn't do it. What about Hobbit? Hobbit could've done it."

"Hobbit would never break anything of mine. Never has, never will."

Sharon and Damon were twins in the eighth grade. They both had red hair and braces, but other than that they didn't look anything alike. But they did both like to yell.

Theo and I were sitting at their kitchen table with Damon's broken iPhone lying there between us like road-kill. The glass plate was cracked around two puncture holes very clearly made by teeth.

Earlier that day, I'd seen Theo at lunch. I was sitting with a couple of guys from the basketball team. Theo had been sitting with his pals from the Brain Train. He'd recently gotten a reputation as a middle school Sherlock Holmes after solving a mystery involving his cousin's stolen song. After a famous band turned it into a hit on YouTube, Theo found out who leaked it. Today, at the table next to us, Damon and Sharon were arguing loudly about whose dog had destroyed Damon's phone. Theo walked up to them and said he might be able to figure out who was right.

"How much?" Damon had asked Theo.

"What?"

"How much will you charge us to figure it out?"

Theo's blank expression showed he hadn't even thought about money, but now that Damon had mentioned it, he warmed to the idea. "If I solve the mystery, you pay me twenty bucks. If I don't, you pay me nothing. Fair?"

Damon frowned, not liking the price, but Sharon immediately said, "Deal!"

After school, we'd ridden our bikes to the twins' house. On the way, I filled Theo in on what I wanted. I didn't want to explain it all at school, because someone might have overheard. Sharing secrets at school almost guarantees that everyone will find out. I didn't have to go with him, but I wanted to see him at work, maybe to make me feel more confident that I was doing the right thing in asking for his help.

"You want me to dig up dirt on your brother?" Theo asked as we pedaled through Palisades Park. It was a shortcut to the Currie home.

"No, not dirt. I just want to find out what's going on with him. He's lying about something."

"Sorry, Chris, I guess I'm still not clear about what you want me to do."

"I'm not sure either. I thought you could help me figure out what the next step should be."

Theo didn't say anything.

"Look," I said, "I feel bad asking you. Like I'm betraying him or something. But I'm worried about him. Like maybe he's in some kind of trouble. He's just not being himself."

Theo didn't say anything for a while, then, "Let me think about it." He looked over at me and must have noticed the worried expression on my face. "I'll figure something out."

"We didn't talk about price," I said. "How much?"

Theo laughed. "Well, if I don't find out anything, then no charge. But if I do find out something, then . . . no charge." He laughed again. "We're teammates, dude. We gotta stick together."

I nodded. "Thanks, man."

We pedaled on in silence.

The more I pedaled, the more this seemed like a dumb idea. Because the more I thought about it, the more I wondered if maybe I didn't really want to know why Jax was lying.

As we flew through the park, we both looked over at

the basketball courts. Kids were stopping for a quick game or two on their way home from school. Brightly colored backpacks lined the sidewalk next to the court.

I noticed the gleam in Theo's eyes. Probably the same one in my eyes. We both wanted to stop and play. When a real basketball player sees a court and kids gathering for a game, everything else fades into the background as unimportant.

But Theo wasn't the kind of kid who'd break a promise. That's one of the reasons I'd gone to him.

"So?" Sharon said now, her eyes focused on Theo. "How're you going to prove that Brick didn't chew Damon's stupid phone?"

Theo picked up the phone, tilted it in the light, looked at it from all angles. "First of all, I didn't promise I'd figure this out. I just said it was a possibility. Second, I'm not here to prove Brick is innocent."

"But he *is* innocent," Sharon insisted. She looked outside the sliding glass door. Brick and Hobbit, brindle-colored bulldogs, were playing together in the yard. They fought over a long rubber bone. As their heads shook back and forth, slimy webs of drool flung from their jowls.

"Are they related?" I asked.

"Brothers," Damon said. "But not from the same litter. Brick is a year older."

"Lucky them," Sharon added. "It sucks being a twin."

They stopped talking, and the three of us just stared at

Theo, who was now puffing hot breath on the broken glass of the phone.

"What are you doing?" Damon asked.

Theo stared at the glass and smiled. "Catching a canine criminal."

# THE NOSE KNOWS

**THEO** counted off on his fingers as he spoke: "I need a pencil, a knife, clear tape, and a sheet of unlined paper. Note cards would be better."

"What for?" Sharon asked.

Theo ignored her and turned to Damon. "And I need you to hold the dogs."

"What do you mean, hold them?" Sharon asked, alarmed.

"Just their heads," Theo explained.

"Their heads! What for?" Damon asked.

"I'll explain later," Theo said. He looked at me and grinned. That grin told me that he could have explained to them right then what he was doing, but Theo liked a little drama when he performed his magic. I'd learned that last time.

I had no idea what he was doing, but I helped Sharon gather the materials from various drawers and cupboards. I held a Swiss Army knife in one hand and a couple pencils and a tape dispenser in the other.

"I have note cards up in my room," Sharon said as she

climbed the stairs. "You'll have to wait here. Boys aren't allowed upstairs." She turned and smiled at me. "But then again, my parents won't be home from work for a couple hours." She waited for my response.

I waited for my response, too. I didn't know what to say. I never did when it came to girls. I was interested in girls (*really* interested, if you want to know the truth), and some were interested in me. Some, like Sharon, let me know they were interested. Others just told friends who told friends who told friends until someone told me. But all I ever did was smile and nod and pretend I didn't notice anything. The rumor around school was that I had a secret girlfriend who attended another school and that was why I didn't flirt with any of the girls at our school. It wasn't true, of course, but I never tried to correct it. To be honest, it kind of took the pressure off me.

"I don't want to break any house rules," I said to Sharon. For a moment she looked disappointed, then she smiled brightly, as if by refusing to go against her parents' wishes I had proven that I was even better than she'd first thought.

She bounced up the stairs, her red ponytail flopping up and down.

When we returned to the kitchen with the supplies, Theo was taking an extreme close-up photo of Hobbit's nose. Damon held his dog's head steady while Theo snapped a couple more shots. When he was done, he took a few of Brick's nose.

Then he sat at the table and used the knife to shave the graphite from the pencil, making a small pile of black dust on a note card.

"Okay, Theo," Sharon said impatiently. "Tell us what the heck you're doing."

"Detective work," Theo replied, squinting at the pencil point as he scraped the knife blade across the graphite. "You know that every person has unique fingerprints, right?"

"Yeah, we watch *CSI* and *NCIS*," Damon said. "You got one of those blue light things?"

"They're called a forensic light source, and I don't need one." Satisfied that his pile of graphite dust was now big enough, Theo slowly lifted the note card, careful not to spill any. "Just as each person has unique fingerprints, dogs have unique nose prints."

"That's stupid!" Sharon said with a disbelieving frown.

"It's true," Theo said. He lowered the note card until it hovered over the broken iPhone glass. Then he gently sprinkled the black dust over the glass. When he'd emptied the card, he softly blew across the top of the glass, spreading the black dust evenly.

The three of us watched him without saying a word.

Theo placed a strip of clear plastic tape across the bottom of the screen. When he peeled it back, the tape lifted all the black dust. He then pressed the dirty tape across a blank note card. He repeated this action until he'd completely re-created the face of the iPhone onto a note card.

He held up the note card for Sharon and Damon to see. "And that is the nose print of our phone chewer." A clear dog nose pattern was revealed in the black pencil shavings.

Theo pulled out his own phone and displayed one of the photos. He enlarged it so he could see the dog's nose pattern. He did the same with the photo of the other dog. We went back and forth a couple times.

"Well?" Sharon demanded. "Which dog did it?"

Theo looked sadly at Damon. "Sorry, dude. Looks like Hobbit broke your phone."

"I told you!" Sharon said. She squatted down beside Brick and briskly petted him. "See, baby Brick, I knew you were the good dog."

Damon looked stunned for a moment. Then he shrugged, stooped down, hugged Hobbit, and said, "You're still my good boy, aren't ya?" Hobbit drooled his answer.

Theo and I looked at each other and shrugged.

As we climbed onto our bikes, Damon handed Theo a twenty-dollar bill. "Thanks, man," he said.

"No problem," Theo said, pocketing the money.

We started pedaling away. Sharon waved from the front stoop. "Now you know where I live," she hollered after us, smiling directly at me.

"Looks like you made a new friend," Theo teased.

I didn't say anything.

"You know," Theo said, "not talking about things doesn't actually make them disappear."

I know, I thought. But I didn't say it out loud.

# GREAT EXPECTATIONS
## (LEAD TO GREAT DISAPPOINTMENT)

**AS SOON** as I walked through the door into my house, my parents rushed at me with their "we have company, so act happy" smiles frozen on their faces.

"Chris, we have a surprise for you," my mom said. She pulled me into a hug and whispered into my ear, "She's considered the best in the county and is costing us a fortune, so be nice."

My dad just smiled and gave me an awkward thumbs-up, like he'd just read about the gesture in *Time* magazine and was trying it out for the first time. The way he did it looked like he was about to start sucking his thumb.

I don't want you to get the wrong idea. My parents are pretty cool when it comes to caring about me. I've never felt anything but unconditional love from them. Yes, they have expectations. Yes, they want me to be the best version of myself that I can be. And that can be massively annoying. The fact that I have to hide parts of who I am from them because I know they'd disapprove is painful.

But I get where they're coming from.

They're both overachievers who excelled in school and

now excel at being lawyers. They love what they do, they love each other, and they love Jax and me. In their minds, they found the perfect formula for success and happiness. And they want Jax and me to follow their formula, because they think it will make us as happy as they are. I thought Jax was doing just that, and the formula was working for him. Which left me as the oddball of the family. I had no interest in law; I barely had interest in finishing high school. The only things I actually liked doing were playing basketball and working on my comics.

Jax dropping out of the Richards Foolproof Formula for Success and True Happiness must have scared the bleached teeth out of my parents. I had to admit, it even scared me a little. I mean, I'd always figured that if everything else failed, I'd always have the Richards Formula to fall back on. But if it didn't work for Jax, how could it possibly work for me?

Which is why I was now being introduced to Hannah Selby. The best (something) in Orange County.

"Hi," I said as we shook hands.

Hannah was about my height, five feet eleven, tall for a girl. She was in her early twenties, though her pale blue eyes were so piercing when they stared at me that she seemed older. She was that rare California blonde who was actually born that way. I could tell, because her hair was nearly white from the sun. She even smelled like sunscreen. She reminded me of a younger Pepper Potts, Iron Man's girlfriend in the movies. Except she had a little scar under her left eye that was shaped like a long comma. I tried not to look at it, but I couldn't help myself.

"Fencing accident," she said, touching her scar. "I used to fence in college. I was showing my little sister how to do it, not noticing that she'd accidentally knocked off the protective tip." She shrugged. "That's what little sisters are for, I guess. To remind us to be more careful."

"Little brothers, too," a voice said. Jax closed the front door behind him. "Hey, Hannah. What's new at the zoo?"

Jax knows her?

"Hi, Jax," Hannah said stiffly. She pronounced his name like it was something nasty she'd stepped in and couldn't scrape off her shoe. Okay, some bad history there.

I could smell beer on Jax's breath. From Mom and Dad's sour expressions, so could they.

Mom stepped forward, took Jax by the arm, and walked him toward the stairs. "I'm sure you'd like to freshen up a bit, Jax. Then Dad and I would like to hear all about your day."

Jax snorted as he climbed the stairs. "Sure, Mom. I'll tell you about how me, Bucky, and Tommy hung out at the malt shop reading Archie comics and playing punch buggy all day."

I watched him climb the stairs, my jaw literally hanging open. I'd never seen Jax be such a smart-mouth before. My dad glared after him, barely able to contain his anger. But we had a guest, and that took precedence over yelling at Jax.

"So," Hannah said, her warm smile back in place, "your mom and dad say you need a little help with math and science."

More than a little, I thought. But I said, "I guess."

We heard the shower turn on upstairs. Then we heard Jax singing an oldies rock song I'd heard when driving with Dad. The group was the Zombies and the song was "Tell Her No." "'Tell her no, no, no, no . . .'" There were a whole lot more no's, which he screeched loudly.

"Why don't we go into the living room," Mom said. "I'm sure we'll be more comfortable there."

"That's okay, Ms. Richards," Hannah said. "I should be on my way. I just wanted to stop by, meet my newest pupil, and set up a schedule." She took out a small planner and a pen. "Now, how many days a week do you want me here?"

"What do you suggest?" Mom said.

Hannah shrugged. "I'll know better after our first session. Will you or Mr. Richards be home during these sessions?"

"I'm not sure. Some days we both work late. Will that be a problem?"

"Not for me. Sometimes students work better without distractions. They can focus more."

They kept talking about me as if I were some wounded bird that had to be nursed back to health even though I might never fly again.

"'Tell her no, no, no, no, no, no, no, no . . .'" Jax sang.

I wished I'd said that.

# THE FAVOR

**"IT'S** just a little favor, Chris," Jax said. "A favor for your beloved older brother. Is that asking so much?"

I didn't say anything. I was sitting at my desk trying to answer Mr. Laubaugh's study questions for *The Catcher in the Rye.*

*Of what significance is it to Holden that Jane keeps her kings in the back row during checkers?* I'd wondered the same thing. Holden keeps talking about this girl he knew who never moved her kings from the back row when she played checkers because she thought they looked good there. Why wouldn't she just use them to beat the other player? It's like stealing the ball, dribbling the full length of the court with no one around, then not taking the shot until the other team gets downcourt. Was she just crazy?

"Come on, bro," Jax persisted. He was lying on my bed, spinning a basketball on his fingertips. "You love playing basketball, and I owe this guy a favor. What's the big deal?"

"I have homework, Jax. Can we discuss this later?"

"Nope. He's expecting my call." He sat up without disturbing the ball's spin. He slapped it a couple times on the side and it spun faster. "I sorta promised him."

"Not my problem," I said.

He chuckled. "Oooh, tough guy, huh?" He let the ball drop onto his lap and beat it like a drum. "Listen, man, I just need you to do this one thing. I think we agree that I've done plenty of favors for you. Don't make me embarrass you by listing them."

It was true. He'd never turned down doing a favor for me. He owed his life to me, after all. But I'd never held that over his head, and I wouldn't have turned down Old Jax. But this New Jax worried me. He was mysterious and secretive.

"Why is it so important?" I asked. "Is this the same guy I saw you giving money to?"

Jax looked surprised, then embarrassed. "I owed him some money. No big deal."

"Why did you owe him money?"

Jax reached over and picked up my copy of *The Catcher in the Rye*. "Aren't you too young for this? It has dirty words. And mature themes."

I grabbed the book out of his hands. "It's Advanced English. We had to get parental approval."

"That's what we're all trying to get around here, isn't it? Parental approval?"

"Wow," I said, "that's so deep. No wonder you went to

Stanford. Must be where you learned to avoid answering my questions."

He sighed and said in a soft voice, "Must be." He bent over the basketball, his forehead touching it like it was cooling his face.

"You never used to be so evasive, Jax. I could always count on you for the truth. What the heck happened at Stanford to change you?"

Jax didn't look at me for a while. He just rolled his head side to side across the ball. Then he sat up straight and looked at me with a sad expression. "I made a bet with the guy and I lost. I don't have enough to pay him, and he's not the kind of guy who just says, 'Pay me whenever.'"

"What does that mean? He'll break your arm or something?" I joked.

He shrugged. "Or something." No joke.

I felt the blood drain from my face. "Jeez, Jax."

He saw my face and laughed. "I'm kidding, Chris. Nothing will happen. Except he'll add interest to my debt, which I'd like to avoid. I'm kinda on a tight budget right now, until I figure out what to do next."

I didn't know whether or not to believe him. I certainly didn't want to take the chance that he might get hurt. "Since when do you gamble?" I asked.

"I don't, usually. It was a onetime thing. Anyway, he has this club team he coaches and they're going to be in a big tournament this weekend. He wants a competitive team for them to practice against. I mentioned you and your buddies. I didn't think he'd take me up on it. Anyway, he said he'd forget the rest of my debt if I got you and your teammates to play them tomorrow at Palisades."

"Just this once, right?"

"Right." He stood up as if the meeting was over, even though I hadn't actually agreed to anything. He knew I couldn't say no to him.

So, I didn't say anything.

"Oh, I almost forgot," he said. He pulled a folded piece of paper out of his back pocket. "Mom and Dad had this out on the kitchen table. I think they wanted to ambush you with it in the morning. That's why I'm giving you a heads-up."

I took the paper and unfolded it. It was a color printout about Stanford University. The beautiful campus. The impressive buildings. Happy students. Why wouldn't they be happy? They were going to one of the best universities in the world. Their future was certain to be happy. Not one of them held a comic book.

"With me, at least they waited until I was in high school to start the Stanford Push," Jax said. He was smiling, but there was no humor in his face. He looked kind of angry. "Next it will be pre-SAT classes on the weekends"—he started counting on his fingers—"then meetings with professional counselors, who lay out a plan for how to get into Stanford, social clubs to join, community service organizations, science camps in the summer. . . ." He sighed. "You get the picture, little man. They're expecting you to wipe away the stain that I caused. Good luck with that." He snorted and walked out of my room.

Middle school had just gotten a whole lot more complicated.

# TWO DAYS EARLIER . . .

# THE AMBUSH

**JAX** was right.

The next morning, they were waiting for me at the kitchen table. Both were dressed in their freshly dry-cleaned lawyer suits. His and hers leather briefcases were standing on the counter, filled with important papers that would change people's lives forever.

My school backpack lay sloppily next to them, some old crinkled papers sticking out at wild angles like unruly hair. Nothing important in there. Nothing that would change anyone's life. Especially mine.

My mom held a fresh color printout of the Stanford University info. They smiled lovingly as they slid it across the kitchen table to me. I could see in their smiles that they only wanted the best for me. Because of that, I wanted to do my best for them.

I took the paper and pretended I was seeing it for the first time. I tried to look enthusiastic. I hoped my eyes said, "Go Stanford!"

They talked about what a great school it was. Sports. Academics. Girls. My dad chuckled when he pointed out the pretty coeds on the printout and said, "Not bad, right?" My mom looked away. I wanted to look away, too, because that was as close to a your-body-is-changing talk as we'd ever had. One time he did ask if we'd discussed sex in health class. I'd nodded, and that was the end of the topic. Thank goodness.

I didn't say anything. I kept the fake enthusiastic expression pasted on my face.

They talked about tutors, consultants, science summer camp. Pretty much all the things Jax had said they'd say, plus a few more.

I cranked up my phony smile to ten thousand watts. Holding a smile for your parents is harder than doing squats for the coach.

"And we think you should quit the school basketball team," Dad said.

"What?" I said. I couldn't have heard that right.

"Your mom and I have been looking into club teams. The college consultant I talked to said that club teams provide more playing time, tougher opponents, and show-case your talents better for college scouts. It just makes more sense."

I didn't know what to say. They were lawyers. I'd never won an argument with them. But I tried anyway. "Club teams are expensive," I said.

Mom nodded. "The one we called was four thousand dollars for the year. But if that will help you have a better future, we're willing to pay it."

Crap! They'd pulled out the better-future-for-you card.

I tried, I really tried, to come up with some sort of logical argument that they would accept. But I couldn't think of one. So I just blurted out what I felt. "But I don't want to quit the school team. I like the guys. I like the coach. We have fun."

Mom and Dad looked at me with disappointment. I wasn't sure whether it was because of the lack of reason in my outburst, or that I was defying their plan.

"We'll talk about it later," Dad said, and the two of them hurried out to work, their briefcases gripped more tightly than usual.

See? That's why I don't talk.

# HAMSTER BASKETBALL

**"THIS** is your best?" Coach Mandrake barked. "You call *this* your *best*?"

Roger and Sami Russell were running downcourt as fast they could. Roger's extra heft slowed him down to the point where he looked like he was running through ankle-deep mud. Sami, smaller by thirty pounds, scampered like a Chihuahua toward the ball as it rolled away from both of them.

Coach Mandrake called this little exercise the Fox Hunt. The players called it the Gut-Buster.

"Please don't tell me this is your best," Coach said, shaking his head in frustration. "Because if this is your best, then we need to find a new definition for the word. Something like 'almost adequate' or 'slightly better than a toddler.'"

"Good one, Coach," Weston said from against the wall, where the rest of us were waiting our turn.

Here's how the Fox Hunt/Gut-Buster worked: Two players stand on the baseline under one basket. Coach tosses the ball (the fox) downcourt toward the other basket. The two players (the hunters) take off after the ball. The first one to get the ball continues to the basket to shoot. The other guy defends the basket. If the shooter misses and the defender gets the ball, they both take off toward the other basket, and the new shooter gets a chance to score. If he doesn't make the hoop and his opponent nabs the rebound, then they have to run all the way back down the court again. The first to score wins. More important, the winner *sits*. The loser goes back in line and keeps doing the exercise until he finally makes his shot. The last guy standing, who never scored, has to come half an hour early to practice for a week to practice free throws.

Believe me, doing the Gut-Buster once is hard enough. Doing it two or three times can leave your mouth tasting like everything you've eaten for two days. Not pleasant.

To be fair, Coach keeps a sharp eye on the players. If he thinks anyone is struggling, he benches them until they feel better.

Which is why Theo was sitting on the bench, hunched over, wheezing like a vacuum cleaner that just sucked up a golf ball.

"I should . . . never eat . . . breakfast . . . on Wednesdays," he croaked. He swallowed hard whatever had just come up into his mouth.

What he meant was, Wednesday was the only day we had practice before school. All other days we had it after school. On Wednesday afternoons Coach had to pick up his kids from their school because that was the day his wife, a surgeon, performed all her arthroscopic knee surgeries. She'd even performed surgery on some professional athletes, including one Laker, two Clippers, a Dodger, and two Anaheim Ducks. He'd told us that they met when she'd repaired the torn meniscus in his left knee. Sounds gross to me, but he always gets a dopey grin when he tells the story. As far as I can tell, love has a lot to do with lame first-meeting stories and dopey grins.

"Faster, boys!" Coach Mandrake hollered through cupped hands. "My daughter's hamster could get to that ball faster! Her *hamster*!"

"But, Coach," Weston said, "even if your daughter's hamster could get to the ball faster, then what? He couldn't pick it up with his tiny hands. So he couldn't dribble or shoot." He wiggled his hands as if they were hamster size, trying to dribble a giant basketball. "See? No can do, Coach."

The rest of us standing behind Coach and Weston couldn't help ourselves. We burst out laughing.

Coach turned toward Weston with a scowl. Even his goatee seemed to be frowning. "Excellent question, Weston. Do two laps around the gym and see if that helps you come up with the answer."

"Aw, Coach," Weston complained as he started his laps. When Coach couldn't see his face, Weston grinned at us and gave a thumbs-up sign. That's because doing laps was easier than doing the Gut-Buster. He could jog at a slow pace because Coach would be focused on us, which meant

Weston wouldn't get tired, plus he'd miss his turn hunting the fox because we'd have to get to classes soon. Win-win. Exactly the kind of clever ploy Master Thief would use to overcome an obstacle. I made a mental note so I could use something like this in my comic.

Coach glanced over at Weston and he picked up speed. When Coach looked away, Weston slowed down again.

"Is it still Wednesday?" Coach hollered at Roger and Sami. "Is it possible we're actually going backward in time? Am I getting younger standing here?"

We all watched as Sami caught up to the rolling ball at half-court and jogged beside it for a few feet like a cowboy roping a cow. Suddenly he bent over and scooped up the ball, then started dribbling toward the basket for what should have been an easy layup. Roger, with a scowl of determination on his face, chuffed after him like a sputtering locomotive. Say what you will about Roger, he didn't like to lose.

"You'd better make that shot," Roger shouted at Sami. "'Cuz I don't know if I can stop from running into you."

Sami took the bait, glancing fearfully over his shoulder as he dribbled closer to the basket. The sight of Roger hurtling toward him like a wobbly meteor rattled him enough to make him miss the layup. He quickly scrambled after the ball and spun to shoot again. Too late. Roger was there just in time to get a hand up, tipping Sami's shot straight into the air. Roger used his bulk to box out Sami, snag the ball, and start dribbling toward the other basket.

"Now, that's what I'm talking about!" Coach said encouragingly. He tugged his goatee as if each tug were sending wireless energy to Roger and Sami. "Go, boys, go!"

Coach Mandrake was the only black teacher at Orangetree. He also taught music and social science. I knew that he'd played keyboard for a rock band called Justice in the nineties. There were some photos of them on the Internet. They put out a CD called *Dark Clouds Comin'* that had made the charts. I'd asked him once why the group didn't stay together, and he'd shrugged and said, "We didn't know what we wanted. We just thought we did."

I had no idea what he'd meant, but I knew it was supposed to be meaningful. Adults like to say things like that, as if life is a riddle we can only solve when we're older. The thing is, though, we're alive right now, too. We're going through scary stuff every day. We could use some answers now. But good luck getting them, unless they come in the medicinal form of this-is-good-for-you-which-is-why-it-tastes-so-bad lectures. Has any kid ever gotten anything from a lecture, other than how to nod sheepishly and say, "Yes, I learned my lesson"?

Roger was within fifteen feet of the basket. He turned his back to the hoop and started reversing in, using his heft to force Sami backward. But Sami had quick hands and kept swatting at the ball. Once he nicked the ball and it rolled away. But Roger grabbed it first.

Probably the biggest thing Coach ever taught me was

by accident. One time I went to see him about a broken locker. He wasn't in the gym, so I looked for him in the music room. As I approached, I heard this really faint violin music. I knew from listening to my parents' music in the car that it was some famous classical piece by Bach or Vivaldi. I figured he must be playing his iPod in preparation for a music appreciation class. But when I opened the door, Coach was standing in the middle of the room, playing the violin, his eyes closed, his body swaying slightly in rhythm with the music.

I'd just stood there for a moment, unsure what to do. I don't know why, but for some reason his playing made me think of my comic book drawings hidden in my drawer. I'd always thought of him as just "Coach," the guy who taught us how to play better basketball. Sure, he also taught classes, but since I wasn't in them, that didn't count. And I knew he'd played college ball and was in that rock band, but that was before my time, so that didn't count either. All that counted was now.

And now I saw him differently. He was more than I'd thought, and that made me feel a little ashamed. Since that day I'd been wondering about all my teachers. What else was there was about them that I hadn't realized? What secret talents and dreams did they keep hidden in their drawers?

"Chris," Coach said, turning toward me, "you're up."

# SHOWDOWN

**"READY,** Chris?" Coach said, holding the ball.

I nodded.

"Ready, Three?"

"Always, Coach," Three said confidently.

Three was Justin Caldwell III, but we called him Three. He was quick and our best ball handler, plus he had a sweet eight-foot fadeaway jumper that was hard to defend against.

Coach bowled the ball down the court. "Go!" he shouted.

Three and I leaped across the baseline and ran full speed down the court.

No one cheered or called names. Coach didn't allow it, because he didn't want any player to feel bad if they weren't being cheered for. "Besides," he'd told us, "you don't play for cheers, you play because you love to play. You let any other reason creep in and you risk losing the fun."

Our response: "Yes, I understand."

But we didn't, of course, because having people cheer

from the sidelines is part of what made it fun. Otherwise, why build bleachers?

None of this stuff was on my mind as I raced toward the rolling ball. The only thing in my head was the ball, as if my brain had morphed into a basketball. "Get the ball! Get the ball!" my basketball brain chanted.

Three kept pace next to me. I realized that I wouldn't be able to outrun him; we were too evenly matched in the speed department. So I had to try something else.

As we both got within ten feet of the rolling ball, I saw Three start to crouch a little and reach out his hand to snatch up the ball. That's when I made my move. I crossed in front of him, slightly bumping him with my hip as I passed. This knocked him sideways a couple of steps, but he quickly recovered.

"Keep running, Weston," Coach yelled. Out of the corner on my eye I could see that Weston had stopped to watch us. He ignored Coach's warning.

Here's where I did something out of the ordinary. Everyone always tries to grab the ball while they're running alongside it. That's difficult to do, because you have to reach both hands down, which is awkward and gets you a little turned around.

Instead, I ran ahead of the ball a few feet, let it roll into my hands, and sped off toward the basket.

Three was only two feet behind me and gaining fast.

I went into my layup mode. Anticipating that, Three

launched a desperate leap, hoping to block my shot. However, I'd expected that move and stopped dead five feet
from the basket. Three hurtled past me. I shot the bank
shot.

Score.

No adult riddles or life lectures or hidden meanings.
No secrets. No lies. No brother hiding something. No parent pushing you somewhere. No hidden drawers.

Just a ball through a hoop. That I understand.

# LOCKER ROOM CASANOVAS

**"WHEN** you kiss a girl," Juvy said as he tied his shoes, "you've got to really mash the lips. Like when you're twisting an orange on a juicer."

"Sounds painful," Weston said.

"It's not," Juvy replied. "Plus, it lets the girl know you're serious."

"Serious about what?" Sami asked.

Juvy shrugged, either because he thought the answer was too obvious, or because he wasn't sure of the answer. I know I wasn't.

We were changing in the locker room after practice. Weston, who had dodged the Gut-Buster, looked fresh and ready to go. The rest of us were munching on energy bars to get us through until lunch.

During these twenty minutes, we talked about a lot of worldly stuff. Mostly girls. At least the other guys talked. I listened. None of us had any real experience with girls anyway, so it was mostly guesswork. It was like talking in detail about a sport you've never played and didn't know the rules of. Girls were basically like cricket to us.

"I heard you're supposed to be gentle," Sami said. "I heard my sister talking to her girlfriends. They said it's more like two sponges pressing lightly against each other."

"Nope," Juvy said. "That's not true. Maybe that's what girls tell each other, but in real life they want a real man."

I wasn't sure how mashing lips made a guy more manly, but since I didn't have any real information to add, I just kept quiet and finished my energy bar.

Theo buttoned his shirt without looking at the rest of us or joining in the conversation. I suspect he and Rain had been doing some kissing, but he never mentioned it, so it was off-limits to bring up.

"I kissed a girl over the summer. She was sixteen," Juvy said.

Sixteen! This instantly made him our team expert on all things related to girls. Harold Claymoore had been nicknamed Juvy because his dad was always saying that's where he would wind up (in juvenile hall detention) if he didn't "straighten up and fly right." "Flying right" meant saying "Yes, sir" to everything his dad said, especially playing football, which Juvy hated, because his dad had been a star quarterback in high school. "Best years of my life," I'd heard his dad say once, with no hint of pleasure on his face. "Worst years of mine," Juvy had muttered. His dad had grounded him for two weeks.

"Sixteen?" Three said. "That's crap."

"Was she awake when you kissed her?" Roger scoffed, but the jealousy was plain on his face.

"She was cool. I was visiting my grandparents in Colorado and she lived down the street. We hung out at the pool together."

"And?" Weston said with a grin.

Juvy shrugged. "And one night we were sitting in the Jacuzzi. There was no one else there, because my grandparents live in a retirement community and everyone's in bed by like six o'clock."

"Then what was this girl doing there?" Three asked skeptically, like a detective who'd just cracked a felon's alibi.

"Her folks got divorced and she and her mom had to move in with her grandmother until they could find a new place."

"Get back to the kissing," Weston said.

"Nothing much to tell. Like I said, we mashed lips so hard I could feel her teeth. She seemed to like that."

"Any tongues involved?" Weston goaded.

"Nope," Juvy said. "Just lips. But we still text and Skype, so I must've done something right. Anyway, I'm going back to visit my grandparents this summer, and we'll see what happens."

See. What. Happens.

Those three words were so filled with hope and possibility and adventure that the rest of us just nodded.

For some reason, Brooke's face popped into my head.

"Hey, guys," I said, "I have a favor to ask." They all turned to face me with surprised looks. I'd never addressed them as a group in the locker room, only on the court when we were strategizing. And I'd certainly never asked them for a favor. It felt a little like in a fantasy movie when the trusted adviser kills the king and then tries to convince everyone to follow him.

I told them about the game after school at the park. I didn't mention anything about my brother owing money. I asked for volunteers to play.

"Aw, dude," Weston said. "I've got guitar lessons after school."

Roger said, "Count me in, bro. I love to crush club teams. Bunch of rich brats."

Roger's dad owned three Taco Bells, but Roger still saw himself as some sort of man of the people, the Abe Lincoln of basketball. Still, I was glad to have him.

Theo stood up, his skinny six-four frame towering above the rest of us. "I'll be there."

"Sure," Tom Farley said. "But I've got to be home by four thirty to walk the dog."

I nodded thanks and turned to the others.

"No can do," Juvy said. "My dad's got me on a strict schedule until I get my grades up. No park, no movies, no TV, no Xbox. It's worse than prison."

Sami and Three also had other plans but seemed sincerely sorry.

"No problem, guys," I said. "I know it's short notice." I only had four guys, but I felt confident I could pick someone else up during the day.

The warning bell for first period rang and we scrambled for class. I texted my brother: *Game on*.

# MAKE IT RAIN

**"HAVE** you found out anything about my brother?" I asked Theo as we walked to English class.

"Not yet. I was going to go down to Dad's station this afternoon and try to make a few calls on their phone. When the caller ID shows the police department, people are more likely to answer."

"Sounds risky," I said. From what I knew of Officer Rollins, he would not appreciate Theo doing anything sneaky at the station.

Theo shrugged. "It's for a good cause. Anyway, now I can't go until tomorrow, since I promised to play on your team at the park."

Crap! Theo wasn't the best athlete, despite his height, but he was a steady rebounder and played with a lot of enthusiasm. Losing him would really hurt the team. Even though I knew it was just for practice, I still wanted to win.

But I wanted to know what was up with Jax even more.

"No," I said. "Do it today. I'll find someone else to play. This is more important."

"Okay," Theo said. "I can ask Rain to play in my place."

"Yeah, that'll work," I said. Rain was a better player than Theo, so it was actually an upgrade. She was fast, a good passer, knew how to pick and roll, and had a quick release of her shots. Guys who didn't know her usually gave her room at first, and she made them pay.

"I'll call you tonight with whatever info I get," Theo said.

I nodded and we both walked into English class. Brooke glanced up when we entered, then quickly looked down again at her book, as if we weren't worth noticing. For some reason, that made me smile.

Stupid, I know. But still, there it was.

# WHEN IS A HOLE NOT A HOLE?

**"RIDDLE** of the day," Mr. Laubaugh said. He held up a DVD of *The Breakfast Club.* "This is the prize. It got me through a rough and tumultuous puberty. I reluctantly part with it in the name of higher education."

"'A brain, an athlete, a basket case, a princess, and a criminal,'" Clancy quoted.

"That's right," Mr. Laubaugh said.

"Kinda like us," Clancy said.

"Yeah," Clancy's pal, Dirk, said, "with you as the basket case."

They both chuckled and bumped fists.

It occurred to me for the first time that I had never bumped fists with anyone. I mean, I had obliged when they'd stuck their fists out expectantly. But I'd never instigated one, never offered my fist first. I'd shaken hands with people when introduced, just as my parents had taught me to do. But the fist bump was different, more personal, implying friendship or acknowledging a shared moment.

I started to imagine a superhero called Fist-Bump, whose slightest knuckle bump could shatter buildings.

Mr. Laubaugh interrupted, "Okay, here's the riddle. Everybody take out your pencil and paper, because there will be math."

A collective groan rose from the students, myself included.

"Here we go: A gravedigger digs a hole in the ground that's two feet by six feet by six feet. How much dirt is in the hole?"

I jotted down the numbers.

Without having written anything at all, Theo and Brooke shouted out in unison, "Seventy-two square feet."

Everyone put their pencils down in defeat.

"That was fast," Mr. Laubaugh said.

"I believe I was slightly faster," Brooke said.

A few students protested that Theo was faster or at least just as fast. Brooke ignored them and stared at Mr. Laubaugh for a ruling. He fanned himself with the DVD as if trying to decide.

"Break it in half," Clancy quipped. "Like King Solomon did with the baby."

"He didn't cut the baby in half, genius," Brooke said to Clancy. "He only threatened to."

I laughed. I didn't mean to. It just came out. But I couldn't take it back.

It was so unusual that everyone turned to look at me.

Brooke's eyes flared, widening as if to allow more of her death ray to fire across the room at me.

"Chris?" Mr. Laubaugh said. "Do you want to comment?"

Not really, I thought. I want to run to the gym and shoot free throws until this knot in my gut goes away.

I shook my head. "Nope."

But Mr. Laubaugh didn't look away from me. He waited. Everyone waited.

"Well," I said, "I think the answer is that there's no dirt, because it's a hole."

The class looked at Mr. Laubaugh. He walked over to my desk, stared at me a long (reallllly long) moment, then smiled and handed me the DVD. "Nicely done, Chris."

The class erupted in chatter. I heard a "Way to go, Chris" and "Yay, Chris." Someone called me "the Nerd-Slayer," referring to Theo and Brooke. Theo grinned and gave me a thumbs-up.

Brooke raised her hand and waved it. "That's not fair, Mr. Laubaugh. You told us there would be math. That answer didn't require any math."

"Yes, it did," he replied. "It required that you ignore math and think outside the parallelogram. Right, Chris?"

I didn't know what to say. So I said nothing.

"Let's take out our copies of *The Catcher in the Rye* and see what our old pal Holden's been up to," Mr. Laubaugh said.

"Now, *there's* a basket case," Clancy said.

I was relieved to start discussing Holden's problems so I could forget about my own.

# SOME SERIOUS BALL

**"YOU** ready to play some serious ball?" Jax asked. He was smiling but seemed jittery, which was not like him.

"I don't know how serious it will be," I said, "but we'll give them a good game."

"Yeah, that's fine. But can you beat them?" He gripped my arm a little too hard.

I yanked my arm away. "What's wrong with you, dude?"

He took a step back, as if he'd just realized what he'd done. "Nothing. Sorry, Chris. I just hate owing this guy." He leaned closer to me and lowered his voice, even though we were the only two people on the court. "I'd *really, really* like you to beat this guy. You know, just to make a point."

"What point?"

"You know, that he's not all that. Not as cool as he thinks." He shrugged. "It would mean a lot to me."

I didn't know what to say to that. It wasn't like Jax to get all worked up about a bunch of middle school kids playing basketball in the park. But then almost nothing Jax was doing lately seemed like his old self. I hoped Theo was having luck with his phone calls to Stanford.

"Dudenheimer," Roger said, pulling up on his bike. "Where are the unfortunate victims of our superior basketball skills?"

"Coming," Jax said, nervously checking his phone. "Be here any minute."

The rest of my team arrived during the next ten minutes: Rain, Tom, and Gee Hernandez. Gee's real name was Jesus (pronounced Hay-zeus), but people teased him by using the Christian pronunciation, so he shortened "Jesus" to "Gee." He wasn't on the school team, but I'd played with him before at the park and he was scrappy and fearless. I'd seen him dive on the pavement for a loose ball and come up with the ball, bloody elbows, and a big grin.

"Gee!" Rain said with a smile. "I didn't know you were playing."

"Chris said your team needed a little salsa flavoring," Gee said, exaggerating a Mexican accent he normally didn't have.

Rain laughed. "I'm the hummus, you're the salsa, what's Roger?"

"Good ol' all-American burger," he said. "With fries."

Gee nodded at Roger's big belly. "And a milk shake."

Roger laughed and patted his stomach. "You know it, bro."

Tom pointed at Rain's T-shirt. It was white with the word FOREIGN in small black letters. The word was so small you could barely read it. "What's that supposed to mean?" he asked.

Rain made her own T-shirts with what she called "one-word poems" on them. I never really got them, but I thought it was cool that she did it.

"Why's the lettering so small?" Roger said. "At first I thought it said 'forgotten.'"

Rain said, "That's a good one. I'll do that next."

"But what's it mean?" Tom asked again.

"An artist doesn't explain her art. That would defeat its purpose, which is to make you think about what it means."

"Man, I hate that explanation," Tom said. "Same crap we get in class. Just tell us, okay?"

I could see Tom was getting a little agitated. He was a math whiz with straight A's, but in English he struggled to maintain a C. He was the polar opposite of me.

"Is this about immigration?" Gee asked.

Rain shrugged, holding her ground in refusing to explain. Unfortunately, this wasn't good for team morale, so I decided to say something.

"Maybe she's asking us to think about all the meanings of 'foreign,'" I said. "Like, at first, you think she means a foreigner, someone born in another country. But then you think, maybe she means everything that's foreign to us, like how Wall Street works, or most of the stuff on the news."

"I know how Wall Street works," Tom said proudly.

I ignored that. "And we're all afraid of what's foreign to us, what we don't understand, so maybe the word is small to show that what's foreign can be afraid of *us*, how we react to what we don't understand. Sometimes cruelly or violently."

They all stared at me as if I'd just popped out a few extra arms, like Armed & Dangerous.

"That's pretty good," Rain said. She smiled like someone relieved to be understood. "Pretty darn good."

Not really. I knew that Rain had been hassled by some kids because her parents were Muslim and also by her family because she didn't really practice Islam. So she was foreign to everyone.

"I still don't get it," Tom said.

"Me neither, dude," Roger agreed. "Sounds like something you'd say to impress a teacher."

I shrugged. I'd pretty much talked myself out. Like my mom always said, I used words like each one costs me ten dollars.

"*Psst!* Chris!" Jax stage-whispered.

"Where's your bike?" I asked Gee. I'd noticed him walking past the tennis courts instead of pedaling the black mountain bike he'd gotten for Christmas.

Gee scowled. "Stolen. Someone got into our garage, took all the bikes."

"Holy crap," Roger said.

"Chris!" Jax said more loudly.

I ignored him. "Theo's dad came by our house the other night to warn us about that. It's been happening all over the place."

Rain nodded. "Our neighbors down the street got robbed, too. Thousands of dollars' worth of tools. They also took every computer in the house and some jewelry from the bedroom."

"Chris!" Jax hollered angrily. "If you don't get over here, I swear I'll . . ."

I turned. Jax was standing about twenty yards away, waving for me to join him.

"What?"

"Come *here!*" he barked, waving even harder.

I went over to him while my team started shooting. "What's the big 911?" I asked.

"What's *she* doing here?" he asked, glaring at Rain.

"Playing basketball. Why?"

"Why? Because she's tiny. These guys won't care that she's a girl, Chris. They will run right over her until she's nothing more than a greasy stain on the court."

I was so mad and afraid of what I would say that I turned and walked away.

"Is that them?" Tom said. He pointed with the hand that only had four fingers. Well, four and a half. He'd lost half of his middle finger when he was three and reached into a blender. (Did your stomach just kinda tighten into a fist? Mine did when he first told me.) Sometimes, for a joke, he'll give someone the finger. But no one ever gets mad; they just stare at his stump and look confused. That cracks us up. Anyway, he's still a great ball handler and a dead shot from the free throw line.

Roger, Rain, Jesus, and I all turned to look where Tom was pointing. Five guys wearing gold basketball uniforms poured out of a white van, followed by the driver, Fauxhawk. On the side of the van was a cartoon frog wearing a knight's helmet and holding a pool skimmer like a lance. Under the frog, in big blue letters, it said: SIR CLEANS-A-LOT POOL SERVICING. I guess Fauxhawk had a side job.

"Holy crap," Roger said with a snicker. "Gold uniforms. You ever seen that before?"

"I haven't," Rain said.

"Hustle, hustle, hustle!" Fauxhawk shouted, clapping his hands repeatedly. The team burst into a quick run.

As they got closer, our expressions changed from smirks at their gold uniforms to stunned awe. For one thing, they ran in unison, their left legs hitting the ground at the same time, then their right legs. It was like some kind of synchronized swimming routine, but on land.

Fauxhawk jogged leisurely behind them, but with a big grin on his face, like someone who's won the lottery and just showed up to collect his winnings. He wore skinny black jeans, a vintage KISS T-shirt, and a brown leather bomber jacket with so many zippers that it looked like it had been in a knife fight and the zippers were scars. His blond fauxhawk looked a little taller today, like a tidal wave frozen at its highest point. In New York City, he would have looked like a gang member. In Southern California, he looked like a wannabe hipster movie star. I'd seen some of those clothes in the fancy stores at South Coast Plaza. They were worth more than the van.

"They're huuuge," Rain whispered to me, some fear in her voice.

"Yeah," I said. She was right. They towered over us, each near six feet tall, if not over.

"Maybe the gold uniforms make them look taller," Gee said. He looked at Roger. "Right?"

"No, man, those dudes are monsters," Roger said. "And coming from me, that means something."

"No way they're our age," Gee said. "They've got to be fifteen and sixteen."

"At least," Rain said.

Fauxhawk scowled at his team. "What're you waiting for? Go warm up!" He threw a basketball hard to one of the players.

The five guys immediately darted for the court and started running drills. They didn't talk or joke or scratch their butts. They ran layup drills, passing drills, and shooting drills.

"So that's what a club team looks like," Tom said.

So that's what doom and humiliation looks like, I thought.

# MEET YOUR UNDERTAKERS

"**CHRIS,** this is Rand Winthrope," Jax said. "Rand, my brother, Chris."

I stuck out my hand. Rand Winthrope looked at it funny, like I'd just offered him a three-day-old fish I'd pulled from the trash. He grabbed my hand, gave it one weak pump, and let go. First Place Prize for Creepiest Handshake Ever.

"Is this it, dude?" Rand said to Jax, turning his back to me as if I no longer existed. "This is your best team?"

"They're all good players, Rand," Jax said, but without any conviction.

Rand laughed. "No offense, man, but my guys are gonna hunt them, skin them, and mount their heads on my van roof. It's not even a challenge."

My team was on the court shooting, so they didn't hear what Rand said. But I was angry enough for all of us. My stomach twisted and churned like I'd swallowed a snake that was desperately trying to find a way out through my belly button. I waited for Jax to defend us, but he just looked away, avoiding my gaze.

"We'll give them a game," I said. My voice sounded normal, despite my twisting gut. But I was good at hiding how I felt.

Rand turned and snorted at me. "Kid, they're not called the Undertakers for nothing."

"Their jerseys say the Gold Coasters," I said.

"Yeah, that's their official name. But everyone knows them as the Undertakers, because they bury every team they play. What are you guys called, the Short Bus Boys?" He burst into a harsh laugh that sounded like coins being shaken in a tin can. "Oh, sorry, the Short Bus Boys—and Girl."

"Come on, man," Jax finally said halfheartedly.

"Sorry, dude, sorry." Rand shrugged. "It's your money, bro. But when I played with the Wildcats, we'd call this bunch a light snack."

"We may surprise you," I said coldly.

I led my team over to the Gold Coasters (no way was I calling them the Undertakers) so we could introduce ourselves. Hopefully, they weren't as obnoxious as their coach.

"Hey," I said to the first Gold Coaster we came across. Like the rest of his team, he was tall and tan. They all had longish hair that was some shade of blond, as if they'd all just come here from an afternoon of surfing and modeling for Abercrombie catalogs.

He turned around and looked us over as if this was the first time he was seeing us. He didn't seem impressed.

I introduced everyone on my team, and he did the same with his team. He pronounced each name as if it were a precious metal too rare and valuable even to be listed on the periodic table: Danforth, Clement, Lambert, Bendleton, Masterson.

"Masterson?" Gee said. "Like Bat Masterson, the gunfighter?"

"Not so much a gunfighter as a sheriff of Dodge City," Rain said. "His first gunfight with a soldier was over a girl named Molly. It ended up with the soldier and Molly both killed and Masterson badly wounded."

"I didn't know that," Gee said.

Masterson stared at Gee and Rain like they'd just farted in a crowded elevator.

Suddenly, as if they'd heard a silent dog whistle, Masterson and the rest of his team ran over to Rand for some last-minute coaching.

Jax waved us in, too. We gathered around him. "You've got this, gang," he said enthusiastically.

"Those guys are older, Jax," I said. "You didn't tell me that before."

He shrugged like it didn't matter. "Listen up, playas," he said. "These guys are a little older and bigger, and they are from those cliff homes in Newport Beach. They're all richer than Donald Trump. They vacation in Spain and Tahiti and are going to get Mercedes or BMWs when they turn sixteen. While you guys are scrounging for summer jobs at Burger King or McDonald's, they'll be cruising the Caribbean on their yachts. You'll smell of french fry grease and they'll smell of suntan lotion. So how about, just this one time, giving them the taste of losing?"

I don't know if Jax expected that speech to amp us up into some sort of Terminator-like killing frenzy, but mostly we just mumbled some assurances to him and walked onto the court.

"What's with your brother, Chris?" Rain asked.

I shrugged. "He's going through some stuff."

"Who ain't?" she said.

If Jax thought he was going to spark some sort of class warfare, he'd picked the wrong group of kids. We were used to all the über-rich kids from Newport Beach and Laguna Beach and Turtle Rock. Heck, Kobe Bryant lived down there. We didn't have anything against them just because they were rich. This wasn't *The Outsiders*, with them being the Socs and us being the Greasers. Orange County had just about every nationality and racial group you could think of, as well as every level of income. Most of us at Orangetree Middle School were upper middle class, but only because most families had both parents working full-time.

Having said that, we still wanted to beat them. Not because they were bigger, richer, or better dressed, but because when it was game time we *always* played to win. If they had been smaller, uglier, poorer, and called the

Lawn Gnomes, we would've still wanted to crush them. That's how the game is played, with everybody trying their hardest to win. That's when basketball is the most fun.

My team gathered under the basket while we waited for the Gold Coasters. Their uniforms were gold on the front and back, with white piping on the sides of the jersey and shorts. They all wore LeBron XI PS Elite iD shoes, which cost $310 a pair. I'd only seen them in magazines before today.

"Don't look so worried," Rain said to us as we stared at their flashy shoes. "We've got this." Apparently she had overcome her earlier fear. Either that or she was a good faker.

"I'm not worried," Roger said with bluster.

"I am," Tom said.

"I'm a little worried," Gee said.

Rain said, "Dr. J once said, 'Being a professional is doing the things you love to do, on the days you don't feel like doing them.'"

"We're not professionals," Gee said. "We're eighth graders."

Rain scoffed. "That doesn't mean we can't act like professionals."

The Gold Coasters ran onto the court. Was it just me or were they all synchronized running again?

"Let's do this," Masterson said. He sounded like he was in a hurry to swat us like annoying bugs and get on with the fun part of his day.

"What're we playing to?" I asked.

Masterson looked over at Rand/Fauxhawk. "What're we playing to, Coach?"

Without even consulting Jax, Rand said, "Game's to twenty-five, straight up."

"Okay?" Masterson asked me.

I nodded. Most games at the park went to fifteen, but these guys had driven all the way over here for a workout.

"Do or die for the ball?" Rain said innocently as she dribbled the game ball to the top of the key.

Masterson grinned at Rain's short, skinny body, her blue Nike shorts hanging so far past her knees they might have been long pants. Her Walmart bargain shoes. It wasn't that her parents couldn't afford nicer gear, it was just that they were having trouble adjusting to their tomboy daughter. They thought this was just a phase that she would grow out of. They didn't know Rain.

"Knock yourself out," Masterson said.

Rain shot the three and the ball swooshed through the net.

So far, the plan was working.

# WHO YA GONNA CALL? COAST BUSTERS!

**MASTERSON'S** mouth dropped open.

"Suckers," Roger muttered.

"No more freebies!" Rand hollered from the sideline. "You should have shot the ball yourself, moron!"

Rain stood at the baseline with the ball and said to Masterson, "You ready to play or what?"

"Just bring the ball in," Masterson said.

"Take who takes you," I said, and started moving around the court.

The game started off in our favor. They'd underestimated us because of our size and the fact that we looked like a bunch of rejects from a student remake of *The Sandlot*. We took advantage of that by snapping passes around their lazy defense and firing off five quick points before they snagged a rebound and got possession.

"Get to work!" Rand barked at them. "You look like you're square dancing, not playing basketball. The next one of you who gives up a point is walking home."

That was when their physical size took over. They fired their passes around the court with just as much skill as we did. Plus, if they got a fast break, their longer legs took them downcourt faster than us. We didn't underestimate them, though, so we kept the defensive pressure on with waving hands and sliding feet. A couple times we forced a bad shot, but because of their height, they were able to grab the rebound and shoot again. It wasn't long before they were in the lead, 15–8.

If something didn't change, they would win the game within the next five minutes.

But what could we do? They played just as well as we did and they were bigger. Not much wiggle room there.

"Come on, guys, we can do this," Rain said, clapping her hands to inspire some enthusiasm in us.

Roger was huffing from pushing against Danforth, who was big enough to push back, and tall enough to shoot ten-foot jumpers over Roger's head.

Gee was muttering curse words in Spanish as he fought to defend against Clement's spin move around the pick.

Tom was holding his own against Lambert's fancy dribbling.

Rain was doing a good job of swatting at the ball every time Bendleton got possession, and she was boxing him out from the rebounds better than the rest of us. But Bendleton was having no problem shooting over her.

Masterson and I seemed to be pretty evenly matched. What I lacked in height I made up for in slightly better court sense and passing. But he was their best rebounder and I hadn't figured out how to stop him yet.

As always at times like this, a dozen sports movies about underdogs flooded into my brain. *The Karate Kid*, *The Bad News Bears*, *The Mighty Ducks*, *Hoosiers*, and more. And as always, I forced them out of my brain because sports movies are mostly crap. It's a myth that a downtrodden team of ragtag misfits can use nothing but "heart" to beat a team that plays better. The team that plays consistently better ball will almost always win. One of the only ways they can lose is if they get overconfident and therefore lazy. They stop hustling for every loose ball, they slacken on defense.

That wasn't going to happen here. These guys were beasts on defense and treated every second of the game as if their families were being held hostage and would only be released if they won.

So forget all those dumb movies. The other way to beat the physically superior team is through superior strategy.

While Masterson was tying his shoe, I summoned my team for a ten-second huddle and told them our new strategy. They nodded agreement.

First, we had to get possession of the ball. We couldn't afford to just hope they missed and that we somehow got the rebound.

We needed to set a trap. Instead of man-to-man defense, we slid into a zone, which is almost unheard of in playground ball. This allowed us to better double-team their shooters. Like most big guys, they'd spent most of their time practicing their inside game, using physical size to shoot jumpers, layups, and hooks. The double-teaming forced them to pass the ball more, looking for the open player.

They were getting frustrated, hesitating just a bit with each pass as they tried to force a shot but couldn't. I let out a quick whistle to let my team know this was the time. Roger and I double-teamed Masterson, flailing our arms and swatting at the ball. As planned, that left Danforth open. Danforth cut toward the basket and shouted, "Here!"

Masterson saw him. Roger and I lifted our hands in the air and jumped up and down to prevent the air pass, leaving him one option. He took it. Masterson bounce-passed around me to Danforth. But Tom was waiting for it. He darted in the ball's path, caught it, and dribbled down the court, pulling up at the three-point line.

Most of the Gold Coasters had followed close behind and were scampering into defensive position.

Now for the offensive part of our strategy.

Rain positioned herself at the top of the key, just outside the three-point line. Tom snapped the ball to her as Gee, Roger, and I set up a series of screens for her. She fired the three. It rattled against the hoop, then dropped in for two points.

15–10

We pulled the same play twice more. Each time Rain sank the basket.

15–14

"Yes!" Jax shouted with a fist pump.

"Let it rain, Rain!" Roger taunted.

"Time out!" Rand yelled.

"It's playground ball," Roger said. "There's no time out unless someone's hurt."

"Maybe his feelings are hurt," Rain said with a grin.

I looked to Jax, but he just shrugged helplessly. I shook my head. When had my tough, not-afraid-of-anything older brother become such a wimp? Again I thought about Theo and wondered if he'd found out anything about what had happened to Jax at Stanford.

By now, some of the regular players were starting to show up at the park. The Kneebrace Dads and the high schoolers wouldn't be here for another hour or so, so it was just middle school kids. I don't know if it was Rand's loud cursing and screaming or the Gold Coasters' gold uniforms and expensive shoes, but most of the kids had stopped shooting around to come over and watch our game.

The Gold Coasters ran back onto the court.

Masterson stood in front of Rain. He'd switched defensive positions with Bendleton.

Just as we'd planned.

Rain stayed out on the three-point line, moving around it just enough to keep Masterson thinking that we were looking to give her the ball. Actually, we only wanted to get Masterson out of the paint so he couldn't rebound or shoot there. We knew that Rain's shooting wouldn't win the game. The Gold Coasters had been smart enough to adjust to our previous play. But neutralizing their best rebounder might give us the edge we needed.

With Masterson out on the three guarding little Rain, we had to take advantage of the situation before they adjusted again. Tom sank a couple at his sweet spot near the free throw line. Gee dribbled under the basket, faked a pass, then flipped up a little reverse layup. Roger had his hook swatted away twice before he faked the hook, then slipped under Danforth's outstretched arms for a baby layup. I managed a couple fadeaway bank shots over Bendleton.

20–15. We were winning.

# THERE'S FOULING AND THERE'S *FOULING*!

**"TIME** out!" Rand yelled.

This came after Rand screamed a bunch of curse words that made a couple moms over at the toddler playground turn their heads and glare in disapproval.

Jax grinned at me.

"Dude, we're doing it!" Roger said excitedly. "We're beating these robots."

"Unbelievable," Gee said, shaking his head.

"Game's not over," I reminded them.

"Thank you, Debbie Downer," Rain said.

"Nice playing, guys!" one of the court-siders shouted through cupped hands.

"Keep it going!" another chimed in.

There were about a dozen onlookers now. I recognized most of them.

When the Gold Coasters trotted back onto the court, Masterson was once again guarding me. Our strategy had gotten us the lead, but now that everything was back to status quo, I didn't know if we could get those last five points before they got their ten.

Rain snapped a pass to me and I felt Masterson's hip slam into mine, knocking me forward a couple steps. I assumed it was an accident until I tried to go around Tom's pick and Masterson deliberately ran into Tom, knocking him to the ground.

The court-siders let out a wincing "Ooooh!"

"Dude!" Tom said to Masterson, rubbing his palms where they'd scraped against the cement.

"You were moving," Masterson said.

"I was stationary," Tom said.

"You going to play, or cry?" Rand yelled from the sideline.

"Ball up," Tom said.

Rain threw the ball in to Gee. Clement swatted at Gee's hands and arms like Edward Scissorhands. He finally knocked the ball loose, grabbed it, and fired it to Bendleton, who made an easy layup.

"Foul!" Gee said. "No basket."

"Foul?" Clement argued. "That was clean."

"You hacked me a dozen times, man."

"Hands are part of the ball."

"Hands, yeah, but not my arms." Gee stuck out both his arms to show the red marks all the way up each to the elbows. "You hacked me so much my grandparents have welts."

This was the main problem with pickup games. Tradition says that if someone calls a foul, then it's a foul. No arguing. Of course, lots of players abuse the rule by calling ticky-tack fouls every time they get touched or if they miss the shot. Still, the call is the call, and out here we don't argue the call.

"Respect the call," I said.

Clement glared at me. "Respect this," he said, and gave me the finger.

"Is that your IQ, or the number of times you've ever been right?" Roger said. He puffed up his chest and I knew he was ready to throw a punch.

I grabbed the ball from Bendleton's hand and walked back to the top of the key. "Foul, no basket."

Masterson looked ready to argue, but he seemed to know I wasn't going to back down.

For the next five minutes it was more of the same. Shoving, holding, charging. Lots of fouls called. Lots of arguing. But through it all, the Gold Coasters kept making baskets and creeping up the score until we were tied at 20–20.

Their strategy was working against us as well as ours had worked against them. The fouling, stalling, arguing took us out of our flow, which gave the advantage to height.

When I got the ball next, I juked around the court, making Masterson follow me as I wove in and out. Roger set his usual brick-wall pick, but Masterson managed to slip around it and stay with me. I dribbled back out to the three-point line, passed to Rain, and set a pick. They were so worried about Rain making the shot that Masterson hesitated, following me so he could stick his hand up in her face. She bounce-passed to me, I fired the three, and it dropped in with a whisper of net.

22–20.

Some light applause and cheers rose from the court-siders.

Rand stomped a couple feet onto the court to yell, "You lose this game and I'm cutting one of you from the team today!"

I could tell from the expression on Masterson's face that Rand wasn't bluffing.

The Gold Coasters pressed us even harder, knocking into us, using moving screens, hacking our arms. They got a rebound off Tom's missed jumper and tossed it to Masterson, who started backing me toward the basket so he could use his height to hook over me.

But I had my arm bar in his lower back and was pushing hard against him. I'm a lot stronger than I look, thanks to playing with Jax when I was younger. Frustrated that he wasn't making progress, Masterson snapped his head back straight into my nose.

I heard the crack and felt the cartilage shift in my nose. My eyes filled with tears, and blood shot out of my nostrils. I staggered a couple steps backward.

Masterson took advantage of that moment of dizziness to spin to his right and shoot the layup.

22–22.

My team gathered around me in concern.

"You okay, dude?" Gee asked. I felt his hand on my arm, steadying me.

The others said stuff, too.

*Sit down, Chris.*

*Put your head back.*

*No, put your head forward.*

*Pinch the bridge of your nose.*

They were just floating voices to me.

At some point the fuzziness cleared and I found myself sitting on the grass, my head bowed. Rain was pinching the bridge of my nose as I was pressing a cloth against my nostrils, soaking up the blood.

I looked up and saw Jax pulling his polo shirt down over a bare chest. I realized I was mopping up my blood with his T-shirt.

Before Jax had his shirt all the way on, he was marching straight for Rand. "What the hell was that?"

"An accident," Rand said, but in a smug tone that said he didn't care if it was or wasn't.

"You'd better keep your animals on a leash, Rand!" Jax snapped. His face was filled with fury and his hands were clenched into fists.

"Hey, you're the one who wanted this game, man. You wanted a chance to win back what you owed from your last bet, remember? I only did it because I figured you were such a hometown hero, the high school Golden Boy, that you'd be good for it. But if you want to call it off, just give me the money right now."

Jax stood frozen a moment, as if trying to decide something important. Then he just sagged, his fists opening. His eyes were downcast, like a dog who'd just been hit with a rolled-up newspaper.

"What the hell?" Roger said. He was kneeling next to me, but now he stood up. "This game was just so your brother could win back a gambling debt?" Roger scowled at me. "Did you know that?"

The bleeding had pretty much stopped, so I tossed aside Jax's T-shirt. I stood up, too. My nose ached, but that wasn't the pain that hurt most. It was the pain in my gut from realizing that Jax had used me and my friends. And that he had become the kind of guy who owed money to a piece of scum like Rand.

I picked up my hoodie and turned toward home. I wanted to say something to my friends, but I was afraid that if I did, I might start choking up. So I walked away.

"I guess that's a forfeit," Rand said.

Jax said something and Rand said something back. I wasn't listening anymore.

Then my phone rang. Theo.

"Yeah?" I said, more angrily than I wanted.

"Bad news," Theo said.

Was there any other kind?

# EVEN HIS SECRETS HAVE SECRETS

**"I'VE** been on the phone with several people from Stanford Law School. Admissions, the dean's office, and—" Theo said.

"Don't turn it into a musical production, Theo," I said sharply. "Just tell me what you found out."

"Wow. Is this your way of saying thanks for doing you a favor?"

My nose was throbbing and I couldn't get that look on Jax's face out of my head. He'd looked . . . *defeated*. I'd never seen that expression on him before. It scared me.

"Sorry, man. Rough day," I said to Theo.

"It's about to get rougher, dude."

I took a deep breath. "What'd you find out?"

"I told them I was doing a background check for a job and I needed to confirm that Jax had been enrolled there and was currently on leave."

"But we already knew that."

"Yes, but . . ." Theo paused for dramatic effect.

"But what?"

"They said he had been accepted, but he had never enrolled."

I stopped walking. I needed to catch my breath. Had someone just snuck on me and whacked me across the back of my head with a baseball bat?

"What?" I mumbled numbly.

"Okay, to recap: Stanford says Jax never took any classes there. Ever. I talked to three different people, just to make sure."

I looked back across the park to the basketball courts. Rain, Roger, Gee, and Tom had left. Gee and Tom were walking together. Rain and Roger were pedaling their bikes in opposite directions.

Fauxhawk and his team were heading for the parking lot. Jax followed, talking expressively, his hands waving. He looked like he was pleading. Another thing I'd never seen him do before.

"What does all this mean?" I said aloud. By *all this* I meant everything that had happened since Jax had returned home. His selfishness, his squirrelly behavior, his scummy friends.

Theo thought I meant just the Stanford thing. "Well, it means that either Stanford University is lying, or Jax is."

I nodded. It was pretty clear which one was lying. "Can we just keep this between us, Theo?"

"No prob. Everybody's got family secrets, man."

"Great. And I really appreciate all you've done. You're a heck of a detective."

"True," he said with a grin. "But I'm starting to think you ain't half bad yourself."

I shrugged. "I've still got a ways to go to figure all this out before my parents find out."

Theo looked uncertain. "Good luck with that. In my experience, parents have a creepy way of finding stuff out no matter how hard you try to hide it."

I knew that was true, but I hoped this time would be an exception.

# PRESENT . . .

# THANKS FOR BEING A CRIMINAL

**DEAD** silence.

Except for the tapping.

Principal McDonald sat behind his desk tapping a pencil eraser shaped like a chess knight on his desktop.

*Tap . . . tap . . . tap . . .*

I sat in the chair across from Principal McDonald nervously tapping my foot to the beat of the Beatles' "Here Comes the Sun." It was the only song I could remember at the moment, and it helped distract me from the fear eating through my stomach.

*Tap . . . tap . . . tap . . .*

Officer Crane stood next to me tapping his handcuff case hopefully, as if praying for me to make a run for the door so he could show off his cop skills by tackling and restraining me like a calf in a rodeo.

*Tap . . . tap . . . tap . . .*

Each tap of the pencil, foot, and handcuff case sounded like an accusation: *Chris . . . Chris . . . Chris . . .*

"Let me start, Chris," Principal McDonald said softly, "by thanking you."

*Thanking me?!* Did my eyes bulge out of my head eight inches like in cartoons?

Even Officer Crane made a surprised sound, as if someone had just flicked his ear.

"Thanking me?" I think I said it aloud this time. The pounding of blood in my ears made it hard to hear.

Principal McDonald smiled. He had long, scraggly gray hair and a black-and-gray beard that made him look like an Irish poet. You half expected to see him with a constant wind in his hair, a wool scarf, and a gray sports jacket with suede patches on the elbows. Instead, he wore black jeans and white T-shirts with "inspirational quotes" on them. Today, his T-shirt said:

"THE ONLY THING NECESSARY FOR THE TRIUMPH
OF EVIL IS FOR GOOD MEN TO DO NOTHING."
EDMUND BURKE

All his shirts said stuff like that, lots of them by people I'd never heard of. (Rain gave him one of her one-word poem shirts with the word FUTURE on it. Did she mean he was our future, in that we'd all look like him someday? Or did she mean that because he was older he could see our future better? Or that he was trying to make a better future for all of us through education? See how complicated her shirts could be? Anyway, he wore it every Friday.) He told us at our welcoming assembly that his shirts were billboards for the mind. "Why should Nike and Pepsi and Pizza Hut get all your attention?" he'd said. "A lot of people think middle school is just preparation for high school. But I think of it as its own world. Middle school is like Middle-earth."

That got a big round of applause and laughter from the nerd herd.

"For those of you who haven't read Tolkien's The Lord of the Rings or *The Hobbit*, or at least seen the movies, Middle-earth is a fictional continent in an imaginary time in Earth's past where magical things take place. I can see some of you making faces when I mention magic. 'What's the old dude yammering about?' you're whispering to your equally skeptical neighbor. Well, what is magic really but that sensation you feel in your scalp when you see something amazing that you can't explain? That's what we're going to do here. We're going to show you amazing things, then we're going to teach you why they're amazing. And the explanation will be even more amazing. Middle school will be a time of magic and wonderment."

I think he oversold it. I hadn't found the magic yet.

Principal McDonald was a chess champion of some kind, with an international ranking. Theo and Rain know more about that stuff than I do. But his office was packed with all kinds of chess stuff that he received as gifts from grateful students. And the students weren't just kissing up. Kids and parents alike genuinely liked him. Even though I was sitting in his hot seat, I had to admit he was a pretty good guy.

"Yes, thank you, Chris," he said. "Because I've been in school my whole life. First, as a student, all the way until I got my master's degree. Then as a teacher, and now as an administrator. I'm how old now?" He seemed to do some math in his head. "Sixty-one or sixty-two? Whatever. Thing is, I've been in school for over fifty years, and I thought I'd seen everything. Every day is predictable and has been for decades. For example, when Officer Crane here attended this school about twenty years ago and I was his English teacher, I could tell he would end up either in the police force or in the military."

"You could?" Officer Crane said, surprised.

"Please, Daniel," Principal McDonald scoffed. "That wasn't even a hard call."

Officer Crane shrugged, looking oddly satisfied with that explanation.

Principal McDonald focused his high-beam attention on me.

His intense gaze was drying out my eyes and it was getting hard to blink.

"I thought I'd have no more surprises as an educator. But here you are today. In my office. With a police officer. And for the first time in, oh, fifteen years, I'm surprised."

I said nothing.

Principal McDonald stuck a pencil into his sharpener, which was shaped like a chess rook. It whirred for a few seconds, and he pulled out a dart-sharp pencil. "Shall we get started?"

# ONE DAY EARLIER . . .

# SOMETHING I'D NEVER SEEN BEFORE

**AFTER** learning about Jax's big lie, I couldn't face going home yet, so I walked out of Palisades Park and just kept going west until I hit Newport Avenue, a busy street crowded on both sides with strip malls and fast-food restaurants. My smashed nose was pulsating like one of those beating hearts that are always getting ripped out of chests in horror films. My Tell-Tale Nose.

My cheeks had puffed up toward my watery eyes, shoving them into a squint. When I came to a Jack-in-the-Box, I went in and bought a Coke. Without saying anything, the redheaded girl behind the counter also gave me a small plastic bag, which I filled with ice from the soft-drink machine and pressed against my nose.

Sweeeeet. The pulsing stopped. Cool relief spread through my nose and cheeks.

I kept walking, the Coke in one hand and the other hand holding the ice to my face. I got a few strange looks; some people even walked far around me, as if worried I might attack them. But others noticed my basketball clothes and seemed to guess what happened. A couple guys even gave me sympathetic nods, as if to say, *Been there, dude.*

Been there. But no one had been *here*. Here was some mystical Middle-earth place I had been teleported to, where nothing made sense:

## A Quick Map of Here

A place where my brother might never have attended Stanford Law School. But then what had he been doing all these months?

A place where my brother owed money to a total tool like Rand/Fauxhawk. The old Jax would have never even known a creep like that.

A place where Jax acted scared all the time. I'd never seen him afraid of anything before.

Here was a place with lots of questions.

And zero answers.

I hated Here.

When I passed Chipotle, I realized how close I was to my favorite comic book store, Comics, Toons, & Toys. I usually went on Sundays and browsed for over an hour, not just picking up my usual favorites (Wolverine, Daredevil, Batman, Deadpool, Hulk, Fantastic Four, Spider-Man, Walking Dead, Punisher, etc.), but always searching for some new series or an old gem that would inspire me to work on my own comic more. Anything by Alan Moore,

Frank Miller, Ed Brubaker, Garth Ennis, and a bunch of other geniuses.

As I got closer to the store, I started to feel better. I didn't have enough money to buy anything, but I knew that just looking at the colorful costumes on the glossy covers would distract me from the pain in my face from Masterson and the pain in my brain from Jax. Undoubtedly, after being pulverized by some supervillain, Batman would have to pull his broken parts together and come up with a clever way to defeat his foe with the superior powers. Maybe I'd get some good ideas for my comics—or my life.

Then I saw something I'd never seen before.

Something that made the pain in my face evaporate.

Something that made me stop dead in the middle of the sidewalk, unable to take another step.

Something that made my mouth drop open as if I'd seen a three-headed mermaid riding a two-tailed unicorn.

Brooke Hill coming out of the comic book store. Carrying a bag filled with comics.

BROOKE HILL!!!!!!!

IN *MY* COMIC BOOK STORE!!!!!!

I almost didn't recognize her, because she usually wore expensive clothes that sparkled and glittered. She was the richest girl at school and she dressed the part, complete with fancy shoes and sweaters so soft they must've just come right off a lamb. No nylon backpack for Brooke; she carried a black leather briefcase with brass buckles, which looked like it should contain secret plans to take over China.

But today she wore jeans, a maroon hoodie, and a purple Lakers cap pulled down low so you couldn't see the face. No fancy clothes, no jewelry, no black leather briefcase.

She walked quickly away from the comic book store as if afraid she was being followed.

She was.

By me.

# WHEN ARCHIE MET SHE-HULK

**LOOK,** I'm not going to make lame excuses here. It's probably pretty evident that, for some reason I didn't know, I liked Brooke. Everyone agreed that she was one of the prettiest and smartest girls in the school. Sure, that was part of the reason. But there was something else about her. Like, even though she was rich and pretty and smart, she didn't have any friends at school. Not for lack of other kids trying. They were always inviting her to do stuff, join clubs, or just hang out. But she must have figured they just wanted to be friends because she was super rich. She supposedly lived in this amazing mansion that everyone was dying to see. But no one had ever been invited. No playdates, sleepovers, birthday parties. Nothing.

Like me, she seemed to have a secret life.

I didn't want to visit her mansion. I just liked the way her mind worked. The way she knew most of the answers in English class. The way she was so confident when she spoke. How she didn't care what anyone else thought of her, not even the teachers or principal.

Once Principal McDonald popped into English class to

talk about this Welsh poet Dylan Thomas. Apparently, he was some sort of expert on the guy. He kept going on about this poem, "Do Not Go Gentle into That Good Night," about how you shouldn't just give in to death, but "rage against the dying of the light." Which means fight against dying. Principal McDonald was being all passionate and poetic and stuff when suddenly Brooke says, "Thomas was only thirty-seven when he wrote that. What did he know about death?"

Even Principal McDonald was stunned, mostly because, as middle school kids, we never, ever talk about death or dying—unless it's someone in the news, like a celebrity, and then only with the word *tragic* stuck on somewhere. Or in a Hallmark card kind of way, like when someone's grandparent dies and everyone asks how old he or she was, because if they were old, then it's supposed to be okay.

Principal McDonald stuttered at first, then said, "Well, he was writing about his father dying. He wanted him to fight against it. To live."

"Why?" Brooke said. "Maybe that should be his father's decision?"

I don't remember what Principal McDonald said after that, but it was something to quickly change the subject. I don't think he wanted a bunch of angry parents calling him later, asking why he was being so morbid in English class with a bunch of thirteen-year-olds. See, we're not supposed to know about anything sad until it sneaks right up on us, leaving us completely unprepared. I mean, we read all these things in school about racism and bullying, but nothing about the other stuff we're going through. When Peter Parker isn't swinging around as Spider-Man, he's dealing with more crap at home than we read in *Romeo and Juliet* or *To Kill a Mockingbird*. Sometimes I think we'd be better off if English teachers just passed out comic books and showed us John Hughes films every day.

Maybe that's why I liked Brooke. Because of that day in English class.

(And, did I mention how pretty she was?)

"What'd you get?" I said as I walked up beside her.

She swung her head around, glared at me, and said, "What'd *you* get? A broken nose?"

Crap! Even though I was still holding the ice bag against it, I'd forgotten about my swollen nose. This is not how I wanted to look the first time I spoke to her alone. Too late.

"I don't think it's broken," I said casually.

She nudged the bag away so she could see it better. Her glare softened as she examined my damaged face. "Nah. Nose is still straight, so it'll probably be fine once the swelling comes down and you look less like a pumpkin."

I laughed.

She looked surprised at my laughter, like she'd expected me to get all mad and start yelling at her. Almost like she would have preferred that. Now she just looked uncomfortable.

"So, what'd you buy?" I said, nodding at her bag, hoping to relax her.

"Nothing," she said. She started walking away.

I followed.

"Bet you I can guess," I said.

She slowed down. "Go ahead," she said. I knew she'd like a challenge.

"Uh . . ." I had no idea. Guessing which comics someone reads is trickier than you think. Guess wrong and they could be seriously insulted. *You think I'd read that immature crap?!* But I was stuck now. I tried to back out gracefully. "Actually, I haven't a clue what you'd read. I'm surprised you read comics at all."

"Why?"

Oh, man, another trap. There was no winning with this girl.

I shrugged and went to my default setting: silence.

"Do you think I'm too intellectual, too snooty, only read Shakespeare?"

I repeated my silence, only with more emphasis.

"Or you think only cool kids read comics. And therefore I'm not cool enough."

I sighed. "Can't you just tell me and save all this talk for later?"

She almost smiled. She pointed to a nearby Burger King and I followed her to a table outside.

"Want a Coke or something?" I offered. I had just enough money for one drink, as long as she wanted nothing bigger than a medium.

"No thanks." She plopped her bag of comics on the table. It was pretty thick. "Okay, guess. What did I buy?"

"I thought we were past this."

"You thought wrong. Guess."

I tried to see through the bag, but the white plastic was too thick. What the heck, I finally decided. I had nothing to lose. If I made her mad and she stalked off, I was no worse off than before.

"Archie," I said. "Or Veronica and Betty. Something in the Archie universe."

She showed no expression. "Go on."

I concentrated. What would I read if I was a girl? Wonder Woman? She-Hulk? Spider-Girl? Bomb Queen? Batwoman? Catwoman? Jennifer Blood? Scarlet? I tried to think of other girl characters.

But then I looked at Brooke's face. A slight smug smile had crept onto it, like she knew what I was thinking and couldn't wait for me to be wrong. Just like in the classroom.

I didn't want to hear her laughing at my mistake, so I thought harder. Forget she's a girl. Think about who she is besides that. She's smart, funny, tough. Sarcastic.

"Deadpool," I said.

Her smirk twitched. "Why Deadpool?"

"He's funny, crazy, talks to the reader. Lots of pop culture references, which you would get."

No expression now. Like looking at a backboard. "Go on."

"Maybe Sherlock Holmes, because you'd like the challenge of solving a mystery." I shrugged. "That's all I've got."

She opened the plastic bag and slid out her comics, except for one, which she left in the bag. She fanned the comics on the table. Deadpool was on top.

"Score one for you," she said. She pulled out a Batwoman, whose long red hair seemed to dominate the cover. "You look surprised," she said, not hiding her glee.

"I didn't think you'd be into superhero types. Seemed more like something you would mock."

"Technically, she's not a superhero, because she doesn't have superpowers."

"Yeah, but she does stuff beyond what a normal person could do. And without all of Batman's gadgets, because she doesn't have Bruce Wayne's family money."

She looked surprised. "So, you read Batwoman?"

Was this a trap? Was she trying to discover whether I had a sensitive side? "When I was younger. Not since she got red hair."

"She's gay now. Batwoman has a girlfriend."

I didn't know what to say to that. Was she telling me this because she was gay and wanted to see how I would react? I tried to think of what to say to show her I was cool with it without also showing I would be disappointed if she didn't like guys.

"I'm not gay," she said.

"I didn't say anything. It's cool either way."

She laughed. One of the other comics was a Sherlock

Holmes. One was the Walking Dead. She shrugged. "What can I say? I'm just a girl who likes zombies."

"But not the fast ones like in *World War Z* or *Dawn of the Dead*, right?"

"Absolutely not! Fast ones are shocking, but slow ones are scary, because you know that someone's going to get overconfident around them and then . . ." She made a zombie face and bared her teeth as if she was going to bite me.

I laughed. So did she.

"Wow," I said, "we're having a *Breakfast Club* moment."

Oh, crap! I had just reminded her that I solved the riddle and won Mr. Laubaugh's DVD.

See, that's why I usually don't say anything. Safer that way.

But Brooke just shrugged. "Don't get carried away, Richards. We're not bonding. I just like watching you hold ice to your face so I can see you suffer."

I lifted the opening of her shopping bag to see the final comic. She slapped her hand down on it. "If I'd wanted you to see it, I would have pulled it out with the others."

"Too late," I said. "I saw it. It's an Archie."

She sighed. "Not just any Archie, moron. A speculative Archie." She pulled it out of the bag. It was oversize and thick. "It's a what-if issue with two stories. What if Archie marries Betty, and what if he marries Veronica. And it deals with important grown-up issues, like divorce and betrayal and losing one's job. . . ." She stopped talking, as if afraid that anything else she said would make things worse. But actually, I found that particular selection somehow touching. I didn't know why, but it made me like her even more.

"I've got to go," she said suddenly, and started shoveling her comics back into the bag.

I didn't want her to go. For one thing, I didn't want to go home and face my lying brother. I still hadn't figured out what to say to him or whether I should tell my parents what Theo had discovered. I also didn't want to face my parents' sickeningly enthusiastic campaign to make me Stanford material. Would there now be a Stanford pennant on the wall above my bed?

And I certainly didn't want to explain what had happened to my face.

"I draw comics," I blurted out. She was the first person— other than Jax—I'd told that to, and she didn't even like me.

"Oh?" she said. She laid her hands on top of her bag and waited for me to continue.

So I told her about Master Thief and how I couldn't figure out what powers to give him and that I sucked at drawing, so all my characters looked like something you'd find scribbled in crayon on a kid's mat in a restaurant.

"Master Thief, huh?" she said. I couldn't tell if she was making fun of me or really interested.

I just nodded.

"Ever steal anything?" she asked, a strange smile creeping across her face.

"No."

"How are you going to understand the mind of a thief if you've never experienced the thrill and danger of actually doing it yourself?"

"I'm pretty sure Superman creators Jerry Siegel and Joe Shuster never flew or had bullets bounce off their chests, but they still did a good job."

"The original Superman didn't fly," she said. "He leaped over buildings. It wasn't until 1941, two years after his first appearance, that he could fly."

Remind me what I liked about her again? Man, she was frustrating.

"My point is," I said slowly, trying to keep the frustration out of my voice, "a good writer imagines things without having to do them."

"I don't think Ernest Hemingway would agree."

All I knew about Hemingway was that he did a lot of things he wrote about: hunted for lions, fished for marlin, fought bulls. I couldn't chance a literary debate. She'd easily win. I changed the subject. "Did you ever steal?"

"As a kid, I shoplifted some candy from a 7-Eleven. And a scrunchie from Nordstrom. No major felonies."

"Did you get caught?"

"Nope." She grinned wickedly. "So which one of us is the real Master Thief?"

I didn't say anything.

She frowned at me. "So, how does this whole silence-is-golden thing work with you? Anytime you get outthought or outwitted you just clam up?"

I clammed up.

"And then what? People get bored and move on?"

Pretty much, I thought, but didn't say anything. Bored yet?

"I've got an idea," she said excitedly, like she'd just invented peanut butter. "Let's go to a store and you can shoplift something. That will help you get into your character better."

I laughed, because I thought she was kidding. Then I realized she wasn't.

"I don't want to steal," I said.

"It doesn't have to be anything expensive. It can be anything, even a candy bar. Then once you've made it outside the store you can give it back. Just tell them you forgot you had it."

I know what you're thinking. You're thinking that this is a really bad idea. If it were a movie, everyone in the audience would be saying, "Don't do it, Chris!" because this is the part of the story where the good guy (me!) gets caught and his life is forever ruined.

On the other hand (just hear me out), she had a point. Maybe I was stuck with my comic because I didn't really know what it felt like. I mean, I could plan the perfect heist, but that was all on paper. I didn't know firsthand the kind of adrenaline-pumping, heart-stopping, am-I-going-to-prison feeling.

And, like she said, I'd give it right back afterward. Technically, that wasn't even stealing. More like borrowing.

"I just thought of something else," she said. "We can go to the Accessory Depot over at the Tustin Marketplace."

"Accessory Depot?"

"They sell accessories like earrings, bracelets, smartphone covers, barrettes, stuff like that. My dad is a part owner, so if you get caught, I can explain it to the manager. No harm, no foul. Sound good?"

I looked at her bright smile and said, "Sure, okay."

And off we went to my first heist.

# MY LIFE OF CRIME BEGINS

**EVEN** though no one in the store was looking directly at me, it felt as if they were all secretly watching me. Like teachers at their desks during a test, pretending to read a magazine or grade essays but out of the corners of their eyes always scanning the room for cheaters. That hopeful drool forming on their lips at the thought of catching one.

I was as out of place as a quarterback suddenly pushed onstage in the middle of a ballet. Earrings, bracelets, and necklaces glittered and gleamed and sparkled on the walls like tiny fireworks. Spinner racks of flavored lip gloss, bedazzled phone cases, and a bunch of stuff I couldn't even identify crowded the small store so that you had to squeeze around them just to move through the place.

I studied each customer with the fevered panic of a prisoner in the exercise yard who'd just been told that one of the inmates was coming for him with a sharpened toothbrush. Who would it be?

Was that woman in the yoga outfit, who was holding up earrings to her ear and checking herself out in the mirror, actually watching my every move in the reflection?

Was the six-year-old boy fidgeting so much because he was bored waiting for his mom to select a bedazzled iPhone case, or because he was impatient to rat me out to the store manager?

Were the cute teenage girls with sparkling braces giggling over the enormous selection of mustache necklaces, or were they actually giggling over me and what I was trying to do?

Was everyone in the store today an undercover cop? FBI? CIA? Homeland Security?

So this is what being a criminal felt like: Extreme paranoia. Cold sweat. Thumping heartbeat. The strong need to pee.

I swallowed hard and wiped the sweat from my eyes. I also wiped the sweat from my hands on the back of my pants. I was sweating so badly that anything I picked up was likely to slip right out. Would that cause me to be discovered and arrested? Would I end up in jail? Would the other inmates nickname me Sweaty the Shoplifter? What if my cell mates were Steve the Stabber or Carl the Cannibal? How would Sweaty the Shoplifter survive against them? Not to mention Dave the Disembowler or Ben the Beheader.

*Whewwwwwwww!*

I took a deep breath, like I did before a basketball game. Calmed myself.

Brooke wandered around the store pretending to browse. Occasionally, she would lift her dark eyes and glare at me expectantly. Once she widened her eyes as if to say, *Do it already!*

So I finally picked up something, a round copper bracelet with hearts engraved all around it, and examined it closely, like I was thinking how this would look on my imaginary girlfriend. All the while I was wondering if I could get away with stuffing it down my pants and marching out the door.

Brooke nodded encouragement at this new step. Like a cheerleader at tip-off.

When we'd first walked into Accessory Depot half an hour ago, the tall man behind the counter had said, "Hi, Brooke. Your dad send you here to check up on me?" They'd both laughed. Brooke had gone over to the counter to chat with the man. With his light blue shirt, dark blue tie, and shiny black shoes, he was clearly the manager. He looked about thirty and in good shape. His bulging biceps pushed tight against his blue shirt. I might be able to outrun him in a flat race on the street, but if he ever caught me, he'd be able to snap me in two like a wooden match.

I was pretty much against being snapped in two like a wooden match.

They'd talked in low voices while Brooke had signaled me with her hand behind her back to get to work. She'd even blocked his sight so he couldn't see me. I'd appreciated her distracting him for me and was about to jam a pair of sterling-silver mermaid earrings down my shirt when a girl I recognized as a senior at the high school came out of the back room carrying a box full of jewelry. Her name was Janet Slovski, but everyone called her Goody.

I'd heard two versions of how she got her name. The first was that she'd once gotten an A on a history essay, then turned herself in for cheating because she felt she'd gotten too much help on it from her mom, who was a history professor. The teacher had made her stay after school and write a new essay right there in class. She'd gotten an A on that, too. The second version was that she'd gone to a beach party with Cameron Littlefield, a popular senior who thought he was cool because he interned at an alt-rock radio station. When she didn't want to kiss him after s'mores, even though everyone else was making out like their lips were on fire and the flames needed to be smothered, he started calling her Goody Two-Shoes.

It didn't really matter which version was true. Maybe both. Maybe neither. Thing is, when did it become a bad thing to be good? I get that when somebody is really good it makes the rest of us feel bad, like we're not trying hard enough, and so instead of becoming good ourselves, it's easier to pull the good person down. Like with Lex Luthor and Superman. In *Lex Luthor: Man of Steel*, the thing that drives Luthor so crazy about Superman is that he's an alien with enormous powers setting this example for the rest of us to live up to. Luthor thinks it sets an impossible standard that just makes us all miserable. That we'd be better off looking to regular humans for models of goodness, like Martin Luther King Jr., and former president Jimmy

Carter, who builds homes for poor people. Maybe Lex has a point. On the other hand, maybe it's better to see that even superheroes have flaws. Like my brother, Jax.

I wanted to say something nice to Goody, to let her know I was on her side. But once again, words seem to tumble around in my mouth like bingo balls rattling around in a cage, until finally it spit out only one ball.

"Hi," I said to Goody.

She looked up from her cardboard box, gave me a be-polite-to-all-customers-even-middle-school-boys-on-a-limited-budget smile, and said, "Hi."

And that was it. Nothing had changed. I hadn't improved her life.

So I went back to trying to steal and she went back to stocking shelves.

And now I had two sets of eyes to worry about, not to mention all the customers who were pretending to ignore me.

Which is why, after almost thirty minutes, I was still skulking around and Brooke was glaring at me to *Get it done already, moron!* Her glares were very articulate.

She was right. In terms of sweat alone, I was losing more moisture than my body could bear. I felt like I'd been playing full-court basketball for three hours instead of walking around an accessory store for thirty minutes. I was probably two pounds lighter than when I'd arrived.

That's when it occurred to me.

WWMTD?

What Would Master Thief Do?

I was pretty good at planning crimes. In my comics I'm always figuring every larcenous move, down to the last detail. Actually, planning a heist isn't much different from coming up with a game plan to beat an opposing basketball team. Just look at their strengths and weaknesses and act accordingly. For years, I'd been walking into stores and banks, figuring out their security, imagining various ways to rob the places so I could write about it for Master Thief. Once I'd confessed my love of comics to Jax and shown him my stories, he'd started driving me to various locations. Afterward, he'd take me out for ice cream sundaes and play cop to my robber, trying to poke holes in my plans. He made a pretty good cop, too, finding every weakness and forcing me to come up with something even better. I missed those times more than I wanted him to know.

So why had I walked in here without thinking things through, mapping the place out first, observing every tiny detail, and then coming up with a plan? Instead, I'd allowed Brooke to pressure me into doing the heist (okay, it's shoplifting trinkets, but I'm calling it a heist anyway). She'd picked the time and place and was even acting as my accomplice.

WWMTD?

Take control of the situation.

I looked around the store. It didn't take long to spot the security cameras in the corners. That's because they wanted you to see those. They were meant to discourage the amateur thief short on allowance or looking for a thrill. The real danger was the hidden security cameras in the ceilings. (Part of my research for my Master Thief comic was reading about security systems. A lot.) There would be one above the cashier island in the middle of the store, in order to keep an eye on the cash register, making sure the employees weren't pocketing any cash. And there would be two fisheye lenses—one at the front of the store above the entrance door, and one at the back above the rear exit. That covered almost all the store.

Almost.

I put the copper bracelet back and waited. I couldn't wait much longer or I would be suspicious just for being in here so long. Most guys didn't tend to dawdle in accessories stores.

Brooke looked up from the display of colorful earbuds and screwed up her face into a combination glare and frown that meant, *Are you the lamest boy in the world?* Or something like that.

I ignored her and inspected some earrings that had both peace symbols and tiny silver guns. I guess it was meant to be ironic or something.

It was weird, but I no longer felt shaky or had to pee. I'd stopped sweating. I was still scared, but in a different way. In a way that was exciting. Like when I'm dribbling down the court and the double team is clamping on me, and my teammates are all being swarmed, and suddenly

I see just the tiniest possible opening. Maybe, just maybe, if I juke to the right and spin to the left and duck under and pivot twice . . . In real life, that almost never works, but that tingly feeling you have when you see it all, know it's probably going to fail, but decide to try it anyway . . . that's how I felt.

That's how Master Thief would feel.

And we both liked it.

Then what I'd been waiting for happened. The manager and Goody were both ringing up sales for customers at the same time. Yoga Lady had decided earrings that looked like gold suns were right for her. And the two Giggly Girls each bought matching mustache necklaces that made them BFFs. Then they saw a fishbowl filled with various-flavored lip gloss and couldn't decide which flavors would be best. Goody cheerfully explained the flavors to them. "The Dreamsicle tastes like a fifty-fifty ice cream bar," Goody said.

That's when I walked over to the one-foot strip on the wall that was a blind spot from the security cameras and from the manager and Goody. I lifted both hands as if trying to grab the stuffed blue monkey from the top shelf. As I reached high, I used my right hand to brush three pairs of earrings into my left arm sleeve. The small squares of plastic they were attached to slid down the sleeve of my hoodie, feeling like hard-shelled insects skittering against my skin. When they reached my armpit, I clamped down, pinning all three pairs under my arm. Then I stuck my hand in my pocket, twisted slightly, and let them slide back down my arm and into the pocket of my hoodie.

Master Thief had scored!

Brooke was trying on a barrette with a big yellow flower attached. It was way too cheerful for her taste, yet it looked good on her. I quickly grabbed her comic book bag from the counter and said, "Time to go."

"You done shopping?" she asked in way that let me know what she really meant: had I chickened out?

"Done," I said.

She smiled, took her bag of comics from me, and I picked up my backpack from the front of the store, where there was a sign ordering customers to leave them. Together we nonchalantly walked out of the store and into the bustling noise of the mall.

It could have been a cool slow-motion movie moment, like in *Ocean's 11*, *12*, and *13*, when they bust the casinos.

Except . . .

Except the manager followed us out the door and grabbed my arm.

He was just as strong as I'd thought he'd be. There would be no pulling free from that grip and making a run for it.

# CAUGHT?

**"EXCUSE** me, sir," the manager said firmly. I could smell his peppermint breath mint and tangy Axe body spray. He had a three-day stubble. He seemed like the kind of guy who always had a three-day stubble, like he imagined himself living in a cologne ad.

"Yes?" I said innocently. "Did I drop something?"

His answer was to tighten his grip on my arm until the bones shifted.

Touché.

"I'm going to have to search you, sir," he said. His grip was making my arm go numb.

My mind suddenly started wondering: what would I call him if he were a supervillain?

Miami Vice Grip?

Edward Pliershands?

The Crushinator?

Rumple-stubble-skin?

"Sir, please turn out your pockets," he insisted.

"I don't understand," I said, furrowing my brow to show confusion.

"You were observed shoplifting."

I gasped, just like on TV, when joggers discover a body in the brush. It's not that hard to do and does add nice dramatic flair. Being a successful Master Thief requires some basic acting skills.

"There must be some mistake," I said. Cue the angry scowl.

"No, sir," he said, his voice getting lower and more menacing. The polite veneer was starting to shed like a collie in July. Even his stubble looked threatening.

"That's impossible," I said, raising my voice. My heart seemed to have migrated from my chest to right behind my eyes. Each rapid heartbeat felt like it was kicking against my eyes, making them bulge like a squeeze doll's.

"Drop the innocent act, kid," he growled. "I've already called the cops."

"Fine," I said. I handed him my backpack. He searched through it and found nothing. He dropped it on the ground.

Mall shoppers were slowing to watch the excitement.

"See?" Brooke said. "Nothing."

"The hoodie," he said, pointing at my pockets.

I didn't move.

He growled, "Now, I'm going to look in your jacket one way or the other. And you won't like the other."

"Trevor, are you sure?" Brooke said, acting shocked. She was a much better actor than I was. Her eyes went wide with surprise and there was a tremble of fear in her voice.

"Yes, Brooke," he said soothingly. "I'm sorry. I know he's a friend and all, but we can't let thieves get away with it."

"He's not a thief, Trevor," she said with an edge in her voice that could have sliced through the mall floor beneath us. She nodded to me. "Go ahead, Chris, turn out your pockets. When he sees there's nothing there, we can go."

Do *what* now? I looked at her with shock. Whose side was she on?

Brooke wagged a finger in Trevor's face. "And I'm going to make sure Daddy hears how you treat my friends!"

"I'm just doing my job, Brooke," Trevor said. But I could see just the slightest smile on his face. I knew just what that smile meant.

Trevor and Brooke both stared at me expectantly. Trevor still had his ape grip on my numb arm.

"Fine," I said. I was wearing my basketball shorts, so no pockets there. I reached into the right pocket of my hoodie and pulled out my wallet and house keys. I handed them to Brooke. Then I turned that pocket inside out.

"Satisfied?" she said.

"Other pocket, dude," Trevor said, pointing.

I reached into my left pocket and turned it inside out. Also empty.

Trevor's face contorted weirdly, like someone had just

poked his butt with a pitchfork and he was mystified about how a pitchfork got into his cologne-ad life.

Brooke looked surprised, but quickly recovered. Like I said, she was a good actor. "There, you see, Trevor?" she said. "Nothing. Just like he said. Can we go now?"

"B-b-but . . ." He grabbed the pockets of my hoodie and crushed them, hoping to find the earrings. Then he started to pat me down, like we were in an airport or something.

"Easy, man," I said. I took off my hoodie and handed it to him. "Go to town."

He actually did. He dug into the pockets for a third time, searched for hidden pockets inside, and finally wrung it like a sponge. I almost felt sorry for him when he handed back my crumpled hoodie with a look of defeat on his face. Then he grabbed my backpack again and dug through it like a Doberman after a bone.

When he came up empty, he handed the backpack to me. "I don't . . . I thought . . ." he stammered.

"We don't care what you thought," Brooke said. "You've embarrassed a friend of mine. And that won't be forgotten."

"No big deal," I said casually. "Mistakes happen. We're only human, right, Trevor?" I smiled with such forgiveness and charity I could have started my own cult.

Trevor looked as if he'd like to do to me what he'd done to my hoodie. Apparently, he would not be joining my cult.

"Just go," he whispered hoarsely.

Brooke started to leave. Trevor turned to go back into Accessories Depot to lick his wounds.

"Wait," I said.

They both spun around and said at the same time, "What?"

"Just to be thorough, Trevor, you should search Brooke, too."

Brooke's glare at me said, *What the heck are you doing?*

Trevor shook his head. "That won't be necessary." He started to turn away again.

"But I insist," I said. "In the name of fairness. Otherwise, it looks like you targeted me because I'm Native American. You don't have anything against Native Americans, do you, Trevor? Does this store practice racial profiling?"

I said this last part loud enough to attract attention from the shoppers.

"You're not Indian," Brooke said. "That's the preferred term, by the way, which you would know if you were really Native American."

"Actually, my great-grandfather was Cahuilla. Or Iviatim, in their language. Means 'master.' Like 'masters of their own fate' kind of thing. They're nearly extinct now." I know this all sounds made up, but it's really the truth. "And 'Indian' is what we call each other. We prefer outsiders to use the more respectful 'Native American.'"

Brooke couldn't conjure an appropriate glare, so she settled for a scowl and handed Trevor her comic book bag.

"Here," she told him. "We don't want to start an Indian war."

"That's offensive," I said. "I think."

Trevor sighed and rolled his eyes. He reached into Brooke's bag while keeping his eyes nailed to mine. I had the feeling that he was planning to bring out his empty hand in a fist, which he would then deliver to my face. My sore nose clenched in anticipation.

Only his hand didn't come out empty.

We saw it in his eyes first. The shock. The confusion. His sweet cologne-ad life morphing into the sweaty life of working the grill at McDonald's.

When his hand emerged from the bag, it was clutching three plastic squares of earrings.

Brooke looked at them, but she didn't look surprised. Or angry. Or homicidal.

Instead, she smiled, gave me a golf clap, and said, "Well played, sir."

I wasn't sure what was making my heart pound more: my successful theft or Brooke's appreciation.

# HONOR AMONG THIEVES

**"HOW** did you know I set you up?" Brooke asked as we sipped strawberry lemonades from Hot Dog on a Stick.

She'd paid.

I let her.

I wanted to give her a cool explanation, something James Bond–ish about how I noticed a telltale drop of sweat on her forehead or a conspiratorial expression exchanged between her and Trevor. But it was nothing like that.

"It just felt wrong," I finally said.

She snorted and mimicked me. *"It just felt wrong."* Actually, if you took away the acidic sarcasm, she did a pretty good impression of me. "Come on, Richards. The truth."

I said, "When we first went into the store, I was pretty scared. I mean, I could hardly breathe, let alone think about stealing. All I could think about was getting caught and sent to jail and the disappointed look on my parents' faces when they had to bail me out." I sipped some more lemonade.

"I hope you're not as slow on the basketball court as you are telling a story," she said, rolling her eyes.

Okay, maybe I was dragging the story out a little. Maybe because I wanted her to stay longer. Maybe because this was the first time I'd ever been alone with a girl since I'd realized they didn't have cooties. Just chillin' and having a conversation that wasn't about homework or a lame assembly on bullying or how unfair some teacher was.

In some ways, talking with Brooke was more nerve-racking than shoplifting. It felt like being on a roller coaster. Not the part where you're plunging straight down and hoping not to vomit into your own face. It was more like the part where you're slowly climbing up a steep, steep incline and you can hear each gear ratchet into place. Your stomach expands and contracts as you anticipate the sheer drop that awaits. Maybe that's what kids meant when they came up with the idea of cooties: that girls had this ability to make you feel like ill, like you've got a bad flu.

She snapped her fingers to prod me. "Earth to Chris."

"Right, sorry. Anyway, then I started to think like Master Thief. You know, stop worrying about getting caught and start thinking about how to get away with it. That turned out to be the easy part." I explained about the cameras, the blind spot, and waiting for Goody and Trevor to be busy with customers.

"But how did you know I'd ratted you out to Trevor?" she said impatiently. She had the same stern look as when she got an answer wrong in Mr. Laubaugh's class and demanded three independent sources of proof that she was really wrong.

"I didn't know," I said. "I knew that you picked the store. I knew you had a long conversation with Trevor while you were supposedly distracting him. Mostly, I knew that you like to win and that if I got caught, you'd consider that a win somehow."

She laughed so hard she almost seemed girlish. "Nice to know someone gets me."

I shrugged. This was the longest nonrequired conversation I'd ever had. Maybe I should quit while I was ahead. If I *was* ahead.

"I told Trevor it was just a prank, but to act all tough and menacing," she said.

I rubbed my arm, still sore from where he'd grabbed me. "Tough and menacing accomplished. Give him a raise."

"So you dumped the earrings in my bag, figuring that if I betrayed you, I'd have a surprise coming."

"And if you didn't betray me, you wouldn't mind that I'd used your bag."

She looked me in the eyes as if seeing me for the first time. "You're a lot more devious than I would have expected, Chris Richards."

I laughed. "Is that a good thing?"

"It can be. Means you can keep a secret." Her face got a little sad and I had the feeling she wanted to tell me something.

Oh no. Please don't let her go all dark and emo on me.

I wouldn't know what to say to make her feel better, so I'd have to leave. And I wasn't quite ready to say good-bye. I sipped my lemonade to drown any stupid words that might want to come out.

And, just like that, the darkness on her face lifted and she smiled and said, "You're a major jock, right?"

"I don't know if I like being called *a major jock*."

"You play sports, so you're a major jock."

"Don't you play any sports?"

"My mom wanted me to play lacrosse like she did. Turns out I'm lacrosse intolerant."

I laughed.

"I've always wondered," she said, "what you guys talk about in the locker room. I've always wanted to hide a microphone in there just to hear what you boys say to each other in your little guy cave."

"That's funny," I said. "'Cuz if you asked a guy about a girls' locker room, they'd hide a camera so they could *see* the girls. And you'd plant a microphone to *hear*."

"A camera, huh? That's a little pervy, don't you think?"

"What's more pervy, to see naked bodies, or to listen to private thoughts?"

Brooke gave me that confused look again, like I'd just peeled off a *Mission: Impossible* mask to reveal I was really an elderly black woman. "Wow, Richards. You can be deep when you want to be. Not just a jock."

"Thing is, I never know when I'm being deep, so maybe it doesn't count."

"Are you really this modest, or is it just an act?"

I shrugged. "Let's go with an act."

She smiled. "Tell me what you guys talk about in the locker room."

"Burping, spitting, farting. Guy stuff. What do girls talk about?"

"The same."

I laughed. "I don't believe you."

"I don't believe you either." She started to get up.

"Okay, well, today we talked about kissing." I looked down, embarrassed. I don't know why I told her that, except I didn't want her to leave. Also, I didn't want her to think that just because a guy likes sports he's a dumb animal not capable of talking about anything else.

"Kissing?" She laughed, and sat back down. "Really? You mean like bragging about the hot chicks you all kissed?"

My nose was starting to throb as if it had just gotten smacked again. Was she able to do this just by talking?

"I can't talk about kissing with you," I said.

She snorted. "Why not? Kissing is innocent. It's PG-thirteen, and we're thirteen." Her laser eyes studied my every nervous shift like a scientist analyzing a new species of bug.

Silence stretched out in front of us as endless as the Pacific Ocean. You could surf for hours on our silence.

Brooke just smiled and sipped her drink, waiting for me to say something.

I knew this was her way of winning after I had defeated her evil plan at Accessories Depot. She'd found my weakness and was exploiting it. In her mind, every second that passed when I didn't say anything added points to her score. I'd never met anyone so ruthlessly and obsessively competitive. I liked that about her.

But I was competitive, too.

"Basically, I have Five Kissing Questions," I said, lifting my eyes so I was staring directly at her.

"Really? This should be fun."

I counted on my fingers as I named them. "One, when is the best time to kiss for the first time? Two, who starts the kiss? Three, how hard is the kiss? I've received conflicting reports. Four, how long is the kiss supposed to last? And five, then what happens? I mean, afterward. Do you keep doing it? Do you wait to see if she slaps you? What?"

Somewhere in the middle of saying all that, I forgot to be embarrassed. These are questions I would ordinarily discuss with guys. (Not really, but if I were to discuss it with anyone, it would be guys.) But here I was bringing them up with a girl. Not just any girl. Brooke. Brooke, who knew a thousand ways to insult you without even thinking about it.

But she didn't say anything for a minute. Then, "Are these questions you ask each girl before you kiss her, or are they general questions about kissing, like you're doing research on Wikipedia or something?"

"General."

"Have you ever kissed a girl? And I don't mean peck on the cheek, but lips mashing lips."

I shook my head. "You?"

"Nope, never kissed a girl."

I smiled. "You know what I mean."

She shook her head. "No again."

I said, "I guess talking about kissing when you're thirteen is kinda like the way a Little Leaguer thinks about playing for the Yankees: someday, if I just really want it."

"Or like discussing a book you've never read."

"I call that science class."

She laughed. "If you paid more attention in science, you'd know that the reason we kiss is to pass along genetic information. It tells the kissers if they're genetically compatible so they can have babies with the greatest chance for survival."

"That's a lot of pressure to put on a kiss."

Brooke shrugged. "My dad says that kids don't start kissing for real until they're like, sixteen, so I guess we have time to get the answers."

"Do you think he's right?" I asked.

She started to say something that I knew from her expression was going to be sarcastic, but then she stopped and her face went serious. "I don't know. I mean, how are you supposed to know? I guess at some point you just do it and it feels right or wrong."

"What if it feels right for one person and wrong for the other?" I said.

"It's like that song in *A Chorus Line*. You know the musical?"

"About dancers. I haven't seen it. My mom loves it, though. She's always trying to get me to see the DVD."

"Well, there's this song about being twelve and thirteen, and the girl sings, 'Too young to take over, too old to ignore. Gee, I'm almost ready, but what for?' That's how I feel most of the time. Like I'm, you know, on the verge of doing something great, but I just can't find the door that opens to that thing I'm supposed to do. My mom keeps saying to slow down, I've got plenty of time, enjoy my childhood, happiest days of my life. Blah, blah, blah. But then I'm supposed to act mature, study for my future, grow up. And I'm like, 'Make up your mind!'"

I nodded. That's exactly how I felt. I just hadn't had the right words before. Those were the right words.

"And now I'm sitting here with you and I don't even know you but you know about my comic books and you planted stolen merchandise on me and we're talking about kissing and it's making me feel weird even though I was the one trying to make you feel weird." She took a deep break and sighed. "I hope fourteen is a lot better."

We looked at each other. I didn't know what to say, but for the first time, I didn't feel like I had to say anything. Brooke had forgotten about winning and I'd forgotten about not humiliating myself.

"That was the longest, most grammatically incorrect

sentence I have ever uttered," Brooke said. "And if you ever repeat it to anyone, there will be severe consequences."

"Your lousy grammar secret is safe with me."

She smiled. "At least my mom would be happy that I remembered that song."

My phone rang. Theo. I debated whether to just press IGNORE, but my curiosity won out over my not wanting to shatter the moment I was having with Brooke.

"I have to answer," I told her. "Family stuff."

"Of course," she said. She quickly jumped up, grabbed her comics bag, and started to leave.

"You don't have to go," I said lamely.

"I'm already late," she said. Then she grinned and waved like a magician conjuring a spell. "None of this ever happened. The comics, the store, talking about kissing, and me quoting *A Chorus Line*—*especially* that—none of it happened. It was all just a dream." And she spun around and hurried away.

I watched her a moment, thinking maybe I should go after her. But the phone buzzed again in my hand and I answered.

"What?" I said.

"You're not going to like this," Theo said.

I sighed. Why should this be any different from the rest of my wonderful day?

# REALLY? MORE LIES?

**"BAD** news," Theo said. "Your brother definitely has been lying."

"That's not news," I said. I could still smell Brooke, a combination of fresh-baked cherry pie and root beer. I shook my head to focus on Theo's voice.

"The news is that not only hasn't he been attending Stanford Law School for the past year, he hasn't even been living at the address he says he has."

"That's impossible," I said. "We've sent packages to that address. Food, birthday presents. He Skyped me from his apartment holding the *Arkham Asylum* Xbox game I sent him. He gave me a FaceTime tour of his place, showed me his roommates, John and Herb."

"I don't know what to tell you, dude. There are no John and Herb living at the address you gave me."

"Maybe you wrote it down wrong," I said. My voice was rising with fear and anger.

He read back the address I'd given him. It was correct.

"Four undergraduate girls live at that address. The lease

is in the name of Elizabeth Graham. I checked with the university and she's definitely enrolled. She's a senior and she's lived at that address for two years."

I was walking through a quiet neighborhood on my way home. I'd stayed out about as long as possible without causing suspicion that would release a barrage of parentally concerned questions: *Where were you? Who were you with? Were there drugs? You can tell us anything. But seriously, were there drugs?*

"Hey, did you hear about Roger?" Theo said, interrupting my thoughts.

"What about him?"

"The Garage Bandits hit his home today while everyone was at work or at school. Got a couple old laptops and four mountain bikes. His dad was royally pissed, man. Those bikes were worth a couple grand. They even took his little sister's bike, which she just got for her birthday last week."

"So?"

"That's a coincidence," Theo said.

"What?" I said.

"That they broke in the week after she got a new bike."

I paused. "Yeah, that's weird. You thinking maybe it's not a coincidence?"

"I don't know yet. What do you think?"

"You're the detective, dude. I'm just a guy trying to figure out what's going on with his brother."

"Right. Sorry to drop the bomb on you, man. But it

looks like Jax is mixed up in something he doesn't want you or your parents to know about."

That much I already knew, so I thanked Theo and hung up. Within seconds my phone buzzed with a text message from Jax.

*Good news, SP. Got you a rematch with the Undertakers!*

# HOW WOULD YOUR PARENTS REACT?

**"OH** my God!" Dad shouted, looking at my face as I walked through the front door. "What happened? Are you okay?"

"It's nothing," I said. "Accident at basketball."

"Accident? What kind of accident? Did the backboard fall on you?"

Mom walked over to me and calmly studied my face, looking into my eyes. "Pupils aren't dilated. You dizzy?"

"No."

"Did you vomit?"

"No."

"Any loss of memory?"

"No."

"Did you fold your laundry this morning like I asked?"

"No."

She kissed my cheek and smiled. "He's normal. No concussion." I forgot to mention that Mom did a year of medical school before deciding to become a lawyer. She said she preferred the musty smell of courthouses to the medicine-y smell of hospitals. She patted my cheek. "And fold your laundry already, young man. It's been sitting in the hamper for two days."

Yeah, about laundry. I like to just fish out the clothes from the clean hamper as I need them. Saves the whole fold-and-put-away step. Mom does not agree with my genius plan. "I'll do it now," I said, anxious to get away so I didn't have to answer any more questions.

Dad didn't look convinced about my health. "Maybe we should take him to the emergency room. Just to be safe. Get some X-rays, maybe an MRI."

"I'm fine, Dad," I told him.

"Are you a doctor?" he asked.

"Are you?" I answered sharply. I immediately wished I hadn't, but Dad had a tendency to worry too much over every little thing I do. Mom was always the calm one, cleaning out my bloody wounds while Dad cringed. On the other hand, when I was sick it was Dad who spoiled me by fetching me ice cream from the store or sitting and watching whatever shows I wanted. If I really wanted Dad to flip out, I'd tell him that I shoplifted earrings that afternoon. And if I wanted him to start climbing the walls and walking on the ceiling, I'd tell him about Jax's lies. Or that Jax had arranged for us to play the same vicious guys again. I didn't even want to think about that possibility. What would I come home with then—broken ribs, missing teeth?

"No, wise guy, I'm not a doctor," Dad said. "I'm just a dad who's concerned about his son. Sue me."

Mom laughed. "If you do, I know a good lawyer."

Dad frowned at her. "Really? Lawyer jokes at a time like this?"

Mom put her arms around Dad. "He's already iced it, sweetheart. The nose doesn't look broken. He just needs a couple Advil, more ice, and a good dinner."

"Good dinner" consisted of Chinese takeout they'd brought home after work. Over my orange chicken and spring rolls I answered all of Mom and Dad's questions about school, even though they were the same questions I got most every day. *Who'd I hang out with? What questions did the teachers ask? When's my next quiz?* Dad studied me like he was my lawyer visiting me in jail and wanted to know if any of the other prisoners had tried to shank me. Mom pretended to be focusing on her curry chicken and fried dumplings, but I could tell she was weighing every answer as a sign of how it would affect my getting into Stanford.

Sometimes I think my greatest work as a comic book writer is the elaborately positive life that I manufactured for my parents. Thanks to my creative answers to their questions, they thought I was hugely popular in school, high-fiving guys on my way to class, every girl's object of affection, and the favorite student of every teacher, even the ones whose classes I was struggling in. In my carefully constructed Bizarro World, girls talked to me all the time, and I had deep friendships with kids of every race, religion, and creed (though I'm not sure what *creed* means). Actually, that last one was mostly true. Basketball brings all kinds of kids together, and I got along with everyone on my team. But I wasn't close friends with anybody. Nobody I would confide secrets in unless I had to, like I'd had to with Theo. No one knew about me being a designer baby. Heck, no one even knew I drew comics.

I was friendly to everyone but friends with no one.

Today with Brooke had been the closest I'd come to spilling everything. But, in the end, I hadn't. I'd sipped my lemonade and iced my face. If this were English class, Mr. Laubaugh would say that icing my face was a perfect metaphor for how I kept people at a distance, like I was freezing them out. I immediately thought of Brooke, how she'd appreciate that idea and I should text it to her—and how I never, ever would. Point made.

Suddenly the doorbell rang and I grabbed the interruption as an excuse to escape more questions about my imaginary life.

"I'll get it," I said, jumping up and racing to the front door.

"Wait," Dad said, as if he'd forgotten to tell me something. But too late. When I pulled it open, Hannah Selby stood in the doorway with a learning-is-fun smile.

She brushed past me into the house and said, "Where are we doing this?"

"Doing what?" I asked.

Mom and Dad appeared in the doorway looking guilty.

"We told Hannah to start the tutoring tonight, Chris," Dad said.

"No point putting off getting those math and science grades up. Right?" Mom added.

I just stood there, forcing myself not to yell at them.

"Right," I said coldly. But the glare I shot Mom and Dad told them I felt betrayed. The way fans felt when Christian Bale said he wasn't going to play Batman anymore.

Mom cleared off the Chinese food and set us up at the kitchen table. "Study hard," she said as she left the room. I could tell she felt bad. Good. She should.

"We will, Mrs. Richards," Hannah said. She unpacked a bunch of books, tablets, and pencils from her briefcase. Then she sat down and looked directly at me. "What happened to your face, Chris?" she asked.

"Basketball," I said.

"Wow. Middle school is a lot more violent than I remember."

"It wasn't at school. It was at the park. We played some club team called the Undertakers."

She laughed. "Really? They call themselves that with a straight face, huh?"

"They're pretty good, so they can get away with calling themselves pretty much anything."

She touched my face with her fingertips as she examined my bruises. Her fingers felt cool and soft, kind of soothing. In a gentle voice she said, "You'll get them next time. It's your house, right? No one comes to your house and gets away with disrespecting you."

I didn't say anything. This was not the first time I'd

gotten hurt playing basketball. I'd had cuts, bruises, sprains, black eyes, bloody noses. And, to be honest, I usually thought they made me look cool. Like a battle wound or something. But this wound wasn't the result of a fair battle—more like a sneak attack. That didn't count.

Hannah pulled up her right pant leg. A three-inch scar like a fat white worm curled around her knee. "Cleats during a soccer game in college. Tore a huge flap of skin open." She tugged up her right sleeve and exposed a jagged reddish scar on her forearm. "Field-hockey stick in high school. Took twenty minutes to stop bleeding."

"This reminds me of that scene in *Jaws* where they compare scars," I said.

She laughed. "That's the best scene in the movie."

"Except the opening where that girl gets attacked and she's being jerked around the water like a swizzle stick."

Hannah frowned as if she'd swallowed a bug. "Like a swizzle stick? That's a good simile—and a disturbing one." She pointed to my backpack. "Want to start with science, or math?"

"Science." My policy was to postpone as long as possible anything to do with math.

"Okay. Get your textbook out. Who's your teacher?"

"Ms. Kaiser."

She thought for a moment. "Then you should be on Chapter Fifteen."

"How'd you know?" I said, surprised.

"I tutor a lot of students from your school."

"Yeah? Like who?"

She named a bunch of kids. I knew most of them. It made me feel like less of a loser to know that so many other kids were also being tutored.

I slowly rummaged in my backpack, stalling. I knew she was hired for an hour, so every minute I burned up with idle chatter and slow-motion movements was one minute less of algebra. "Have you heard about all the garages being broken into?"

"Yeah. Officer Rollins stopped by a couple houses where I tutor to warn the parents." She grabbed the science book out of my hands. "You done stalling? I promised your parents a full hour, and that's what they're going to get." She took out her phone and started the timekeeping function. "The hour starts . . . now."

Turned out it wasn't so bad. Hannah was good at explaining things, even something as complex as the periodic table, which to me looked like ancient Egyptian hieroglyphics. Even so, my eyes started to close sometime during her explanation about gases and solids.

"Hey," she said, nudging my arm. "You looking for me to add another scar to your collection?"

"Sorry," I said. I sat up straighter, sipped some of the iced tea Mom had poured for both of us.

"You know, Chris, I don't come cheap. So don't waste your parents' money here."

"Right," I said. "I won't."

She looked at me and sighed. "Why isn't methane gas on the periodic table?"

"Because it's a compound, not an element. It's made up of the elements carbon and hydrogen."

She smiled and clapped her hands. "Very good. You know what produces a lot of methane?"

I shook my head.

"Farts," she said.

I laughed.

"Don't laugh," she said, but with a smile on her face. "Methane is a greenhouse gas and all the farting from people and animals is a danger to the environment. Did you ever light a fart?"

"No. But I've seen it in movies."

"Movies get it wrong. *Dumb and Dumber, Dennis the Menace, Nutty Professor 2*, they show an orange flame when someone lights a fart. In reality, it would be blue."

"How do you know?" I teased.

"Two college chemistry courses. And a few fraternity parties. Frat boys love doing that stuff."

We both laughed.

"How's it going?" Dad asked, poking his head into the kitchen.

"I'm learning a lot about chemistry," I said.

"Great," Dad said. He waited, said "Great" again, and left.

The rest of the session went pretty well, even the algebra.

Hannah didn't rush me or get impatient when I didn't understand a concept. In fact, I was just getting the hang of figuring out a nasty variable when the front door opened loudly and I heard Jax saying hi to Mom and Dad. A couple seconds later, he walked into the kitchen, went straight to the refrigerator, and helped himself to a beer.

He leaned against the wall and grinned. "The return of the Dynamic Duo, huh?"

I could smell the beer on him. This wasn't his first.

Hannah's cell-phone timer buzzed. "Time's up for tonight. Good job, Chris. See you next week."

"Next week?" I said.

"Your folks have me coming once a week to start. If you need more help, we'll add an extra day. Sound good?"

"Yeah, sure."

"What time do you usually get home from school?"

"Depends how long practice runs. Usually I'm home by four. Why?"

"Just need to know when to add the extra sessions if we need them." She must have noticed the panicked look on my face. She smiled. "Don't worry, we probably won't need them."

She started packing her stuff into her canvas bag. She was very pretty, in an Older Woman kind of way.

"How's it going, Hannah?" Jax asked.

"Fine, Jax," Hannah said, with icicles hanging from each word.

"Come on. You're not still mad about prom, are you?"

She looked surprised. "Prom? That was years ago. Why would I care?"

"Because you asked me to take you to the dance, but I had already asked Tina Mayfair. You've hardly spoken to me since."

"I've hardly seen you since. That was senior year and we weren't in the same classes. We went to different colleges. You majored in poli sci and I majored in education. You went to Stanford and I went to the University of Arizona."

"Go, Wildcats!"

"I didn't have time to attend games, Jax. I was busy working two waitressing jobs and studying the rest of the time. We didn't all have full scholarships. I'll be paying off student loans until I'm thirty. So don't think we ever had anything in common."

Jax looked confused, then a little embarrassed. "Oh," he said. "Okay, then we're good?"

She looked him up and down with the same disapproving expression that Mom gave him the night he'd told them about dropping out of Stanford. "*I'm* good," she said. "I'm not sure what you are."

Jax grinned again, but it was a strained grin. "Ouch, that's brutal." Then he slipped around the corner and disappeared.

Hannah looked at me sympathetically. "Sorry about that, Chris. It's just that I'm a little surprised about Jax. We all had such high hopes for him. Maybe that wasn't fair. Anyone can crack under too much pressure."

Were we still talking about Jax—or me?

She shrugged. "Still, no one expected him to end up like this."

"I get it," I said. "Neither did I."

She nodded at my sore face. "The Jax I knew in high school wouldn't have let that happen. He would have protected you."

She grabbed her bag of books and left.

I stood alone in the kitchen a moment. She was right. The Jax I knew wouldn't have let that happen to me. He'd have stopped the game or told Fauxhawk to get out of the park and take his punk team with him.

But not this Jax. This Jax had just stood by and watched.

I'd been making excuses for his behavior long enough. I needed to confront him right now with everything I knew.

I jumped up and headed for his room, feeling like a gunslinger walking down Main Street for a showdown.

# THE BRO CODE

**I WALKED** up the stairs as Mom shouted, "How'd it go, Chris?"

"Fine," I shouted back, and hurried up the stairs. Parents are like Wi-Fi: you have to get beyond their broadcast range if you want any privacy.

Jax's door was open, so I burst into his room, my face hot with anger. "I want to know what's going on and I want to know right now!"

He was lying on his bed reading a book. He threw something at me.

I caught it in midair. A bag of frozen peas.

"Put it on your face. The swelling's starting to come back."

"Since when do we have vegetables in the house?" I asked. Mom hadn't cooked a dinner since I was old enough to order from a take-home menu. Dad occasionally made pancakes or omelets. Our freezer held only ice cream sandwiches—and Hot Pockets for emergencies.

"Since never. I bought them at the store on my way

home. They work better than ice packs, because they conform to your face."

I stared at the frozen peas, trying to decide whether to throw them back at him or press them to my face, which actually was starting to throb again. I went with my face. "I'm serious, Jax. I want the truth."

I expected him to grin and say something cheesy like "You can't handle the truth" or another line from a movie. But he didn't. He just sighed and nodded for me to sit down. I sat on the chair at his desk.

"I know you haven't been going to Stanford," I told him. "I know that you haven't even lived at that address you gave us."

He stared at me with a surprised expression. "Do Mom and Dad know?"

"No."

"Don't tell them."

I shrugged. "I haven't decided yet."

He sat up anxiously. "Don't say anything to them, Chris. Please. It's important."

"Then tell me what's going on, Jax. Tell me where you've been for more than a year while we all thought you were studying law."

"Can't you just trust me, SP?" He slapped on his big, fat charming smile. "You know, Bro Code. Brothers have each other's backs."

"That's the thing, man. You haven't really had my back

since you got back home. And I want to know why, or I'm going right down to tell Mom and Dad what I know."

"Things are . . . complicated."

I snorted (Brooke would have been proud). "Complicated? That's a line from every ABC Family show ever."

"Good point," he said. "I'm asking you to trust me, Chris."

"How can I trust you when all you've done is lie to us?"

"I have my reasons."

"Great. Tell them to me."

He sighed. He tossed his book onto his desk. It slid across and knocked his keys to the floor.

"Crap," he said. He started to get up from the bed to retrieve them when he suddenly winced and grabbed his right side. The pain was so intense that he sat back on the bed.

"Jax!" I shouted, and knelt beside him. I lifted up his shirt and saw a bag of frozen corn strapped to his ribs with an elastic ankle wrap.

He tried to push me away, but he was weak. "I'm fine, bro."

I removed the wrap and bag of corn. A huge boot-shaped bruise darkened his skin like a giant tattoo. "Oh my God, Jax! What happened?"

"Basketball accident?" he said with a weak chuckle.

When I looked at his back, I saw several more bruises. I got up and marched toward the door.

"Hey! Where are you going?" he asked.

"To get Mom and Dad. You need medical help. And maybe even a lawyer."

Jax jumped up, winced, and hugged his bruised ribs. He blocked the door. "You can't do that, Chris. Seriously. For all of your sakes."

"What's that supposed to mean?"

"It means I don't want to put you guys in danger. But if you tell Mom and Dad, that's exactly what will happen."

I said nothing. I had to think. All this was happening so fast that I didn't know what to do.

"I know it looks bad, Chris. And I know you're only looking out for me. But I need you to just sit down and listen for a minute." He pointed to the desk chair.

"This better be good," I said as I sat. "Otherwise, I'm telling Mom and Dad."

"Okay." Jax sat back on the bed. He grabbed the bag of frozen corn and slipped it under his shirt, pinning it to his ribs with his arm. "At least we'll have a healthy snack of corn and peas after this is over." He smiled.

I didn't. "Just talk."

"I'm involved in something, Chris," he began, carefully choosing his words. "I can't tell you what, because I don't want you involved."

"I *am* involved."

"Not really."

"Did the basketball game today with the Undertakers have something to do with what you're into?"

He nodded. "Only a little."

I took the bag of peas off my face to show him the swelling. "Then I'm involved."

He groaned. "You don't understand and I can't explain it to you. Not yet. For now, I need you to trust me and not tell Mom and Dad. Or any of your friends."

"Because they'd be in danger?" I said sarcastically.

"Yes. It's not a game, bro. These people don't play around." He nodded at his bruised body. "As you can see."

"Who did this? Was it Faux—I mean Rand?"

Jax shrugged. "He wears very thick boots."

"Why did he do this?"

"I owe him money."

"How much?"

"A lot."

"How much? I have savings. Almost a thousand dollars."

"Really?" Jax laughed. "I've never saved more than a hundred bucks in my life. Anyway, I appreciate the gesture, man, but it's not enough. Not nearly."

We both sat there for a minute, neither speaking.

"So, is he going to kill you or something if you don't give him the money?"

Jax shrugged. "No, because then he wouldn't get his money. But he can make me very uncomfortable until I pay."

Tears were starting to form in my eyes. I tried to force them back. This wasn't the time to fall apart. My brother needed help.

"And you thought you could win the money back if

we beat the Undertakers? You had to know we couldn't. They're older and bigger and probably even better."

"Rand gave me great odds. If you had won, I would've been out of debt. Free and clear. It was worth the risk."

"What about the risk to *us*? Those guys were monsters."

Jax looked down, embarrassed. "Yeah, you're right. I got so caught up in my own problems I didn't stop to think."

"So all this is because you have a gambling problem?"

"Pretty much."

"You dropped out of Stanford Law School to gamble?"

"Ironic, huh?" he said.

"Don't try to be cute, Jax!" I hollered. "Not now! Not about all this!"

He nodded but didn't say anything.

"So what do we do now?" I asked.

"What do you mean?"

"How do we fix this? Make Rand go away?"

Jax sat up and looked me straight in the eye. I'd never seen him so serious. "You know how you're always checking places out, trying to figure how Master Thief would rob them?"

I nodded.

"Well, I need you to give me a plan for how to rob a local business."

"*What?!*"

"I need to go in after hours, when the place is closed, and steal enough stuff to pay off my debt."

I slumped over. My stomach felt like a WWE wrestling

ring and someone was slamming metal chairs into my intestines. "That's just going to make things worse, Jax. What if you get caught?"

"I won't."

"Yeah, right, because no criminal ever gets caught."

"I'm not your average criminal."

"Since when did you start being *any* kind of criminal?" The tears were back and I was fighting a losing battle keeping them in. I wiped my eyes, pretending I was just tired.

"I'm not a criminal, Chris. Not really. This is a onetime thing. And I promise you that I will make it up to everyone involved. I swear to you. I just need you to trust me." He reached out and put his hand on my shoulder. "You saved my life when you were just a baby. Now I'm asking you to do it again."

I frowned at him. "Dude, that line's even cheesier than 'It's complicated.'"

"Desperate times call for desperate cheese." He squeezed my shoulder in a brotherly way. "Will you do it, Chris? Will you help me?"

I was still trying to process everything when the bedroom door opened and Dad walked in. "So, what are you guys talking about?"

# MIDWEEK TERROR

**THE** house was dark.

Evil dark. Like the dark when you wake up inside a sealed coffin.

The only light was from a dim flashlight that would start to fade out until whacked against the leg.

In the room down the hall on the right was a creepy moaning, like someone in a hospital for the criminally insane.

Which is exactly where we were.

Suddenly the door on the left flew open and a woman in a shredded white dress leaped out with an ax. Her face was ghastly: the skin burned off from acid, one eye hanging half out of its socket, her thin lips stretched over her teeth like a skeleton face. Her wedding dress was covered in blood.

Fortunately, all this was happening to someone else on the movie screen. Nevertheless, Dad and I crouched down in our seats. We were both wearing sweatshirts with the hoods up and cinched tight around our faces so only our eyes were visible. This is how we always dressed when we went to a horror film.

I wasn't sure why Dad had insisted we go to the movies on a school night. He'd just walked into Jax's room, interrupted our discussion of committing a felony, and said, "Who wants to go see *Dark Evil 2*?"

Jax had declined, of course, but I could tell by Dad's look that this was something he wanted to do with me, so I said yes. This was *our* thing anyway. Dad had been taking me to scary films ever since I was ten. I never got nightmares, so we just kept going. Mom hated them ("I don't see what's so entertaining about horrible girls with stringy hair crawling out of your TV screen"), so it was just Dad and me. We always tanked up at the concession counter with popcorn, candy, and giant sodas. Then, once the movie started, we flipped on our hoods, tightened them around our faces like masks, and hunched down in our seats, giving in to the fear. Dad had spilled more than one popcorn by jumping in his seat when something suddenly lunged out on the screen.

On the ride home after the movie, Dad was quiet. Usually we dissected the film, reliving all the best scenes and recalling how stupid the characters were to wind up alone with a homicidal demon. Not tonight. Something was on his mind. I eventually realized that the whole point of our going out to the movies on a school night was so we could have this time alone.

I waited. I could outwait anyone in the silent game.

Finally, he said, "Are you okay, Chris?"

This took me by surprise, though you'd think that after Jax asked me to help him rob a store, nothing would surprise me.

"I'm fine, Dad," I said.

"Good," he said. "It's just that there have been a lot of changes in the last couple days. Jax coming home . . ."

He let that hang, as if waiting for me to add something. I let it hang, too.

"I know his dropping out of Stanford must have come as a shock to you."

"He's on a leave of absence," I said. I don't know why I said that, why I was defending Jax's lies.

Dad shrugged. "Now Mom and I are dumping Stanford catalogs on you, hiring tutors, enrolling you in PSAT classes—"

"In what?" I snapped.

"Sorry, we forgot to tell you. It's just once a month for now. Later, when you get closer to taking them for real, we'll do it every Saturday."

I didn't say anything. What was the point? Apparently, he and Mom had my life all figured out.

"We've also been looking into club teams for basketball."

This time I spoke up. "I told you, I don't want to join a club team. I'm happy playing for the school."

"Like we said before, Chris, playing club will—"

"Get me noticed more. I know. But I don't want to be noticed more. I just want to play ball with my friends, mind my own business, and *have you and Mom mind your own business!*"

Uh-oh.

My heart beat a drum solo against my chest. I wished I could pull my hoodie over my face, cinch it up, and scrunch down in my seat. I'd never yelled at him like that, so I wasn't sure what reaction to expect.

"Son," he said quietly, "I love you."

Okay, I hadn't expected that.

"And I know you think Mom and I are suddenly interfering in your life because of Jax's screwing up. That's partially true. But that's not all of it."

He was silent a minute, like he wasn't sure what to say, or maybe how much he wanted to tell me.

"When Jax was about, I don't know, ten or eleven, Mom and I were watching this old movie on TV called *And Justice for All.*"

"I've heard Jax quote it before. 'You're out of order! You're out of order! The whole trial is out of order!' He loves that part."

Dad chuckled. "Yeah, he does. Thing is, the movie was too mature for him at that age, but we didn't think he was watching it. He was over at the dining room table, reading some Harry Potter novel. Anyway, the movie is about this crusading young lawyer fighting a corrupt legal system. Mom and I had both seen it in college and it had influenced us to become lawyers." He paused again, scrunching his face as if remembering something bad. "In the movie, the lawyer has a young client who's innocent but gets sent to jail because of some misfiled paperwork. The innocent kid hangs himself in prison."

"Why did he do that if he was innocent?"

Dad sighed. "Bad things can happen to you in prison. Doesn't matter if you're innocent or guilty."

I thought about Jax. About the robbery he wanted me to help him with. Would the same bad things happen to us?

"The thing is, when the movie was over, your mom and I looked over at Jax and saw that he was crying. He was being quiet about it, but his shoulders were shaking, and when he looked up, his face was wet with tears. We asked him what was wrong and he said, 'It's not fair! It's just not fair!'" Dad looked over at me. "He was so outraged by the injustice that he couldn't stand it. After that, he went through our DVD collection and started watching movies on his own. Not the Harry Potter or Adam Sandler films like before, but *To Kill a Mockingbird* and *Twelve Angry Men*. Movies about justice and the law. All he talked about was how one day he would become a lawyer and stop the injustice. That's why we did everything we could to help him get into Stanford Law School. Because that was *his* dream. Not ours."

I hadn't known all that about Jax. I wondered why he'd never told me.

"See," Dad continued, "with Jax it was easy for us, because he always knew what he wanted. He had a passion. But with you, Chris . . . you've never shown passion for anything. Not that you have to yet—heck, you're only thirteen. But we want to at least lay out some sort of path for you. Right now it's law. But that's only a suggestion. If you choose another path, that's fine with us. You want to be a teacher or a trapeze artist, it doesn't matter. But Mom and I want you to be able to have choices. So, if we're acting a little crazy right now, it's because seeing Jax crash and burn like this has made us worry even more for you. I mean, if someone like Jax, who knew exactly what he wanted from the age of ten, could fail . . ."

He left the rest unspoken. But I filled in the words for myself: *Then what chance does someone as unfocused as you have?*

Did it really matter? After all, I had only been conceived to be some sort of life-support system for Jax. My path was to give him a future. Now his future was flat-lining.

During the whole ride I'd been debating with myself about whether or not to tell Dad the truth about Jax. I had hoped he might be able to help. But now I thought it would only make Mom and Dad feel like bigger failures.

I swallowed something thick in my throat. I'd rather get another elbow to my nose than feel this bad.

"My point is, son, that I'm sorry if Mom and I are acting like helicopter parents, or whatever the term is now. But we're trying to make sure you succeed where Jax didn't."

I could have told him that I did have a passion: comic books. But compared to ridding the world of injustice, that would seem so lame. I still hadn't even figured out everything about Master Thief yet. Plus, having a secret is like having a hidden treasure to use in an emergency. Like Hot Pockets.

"You understand, Chris?" Dad asked.

"Yeah," I said. And we were silent the rest of the drive home.

# SAVIOR SIBLING—AGAIN

**"SO,** are you going to help me, or what?" Jax asked.

I looked at him, sitting on the edge of my bed, holding a fresh bag of ice to his ribs. Was this the same guy who'd cried at injustice? The same guy who'd vowed to end it, like Bruce Wayne after his parents were murdered, or the Punisher after his family was mowed down by gangsters, or Hit Girl after Big Daddy was killed? The same guy who'd taken me along on his dates, to beach parties, to Lakers games when he didn't have to?

I didn't know the answer. In the end, all I knew was that this guy asking me to help him rob a store wasn't the real Jax, and it was my job as his brother—his spare parts—to help him get back to himself. He'd promised me that he would make everything right, even with the place he robbed. Given all that had happened in the past few days, I had no reason to believe him. But I chose to believe him anyway. I guess, after all we'd been through together, I didn't want to live in a world where I couldn't believe him.

I also figured that I might be able to control the situation, to keep it from getting any worse.

"Yes, I'll help you," I said.

He sighed with relief. "Thanks, bro. I owe you big-time."

"Don't you ever get sick of saying that? Isn't it about time you pay me back?"

"I will, after this," Jax said. "All my debts will be settled after this."

Yeah, sure, I thought to myself. Out loud I said, "How much money do you need?"

"I need goods worth ten thousand dollars."

I gagged. "*Ten grand?!* I thought we were talking about a couple hundred or something. That's insane, not to mention impossible."

"Nothing's impossible. Haven't you seen the inspirational posters in Ms. Truman's office?" He curled his fingers and held them in front of him in imitation of the cat in the poster dangling by his front paws from a bar. "Hang in there, baby!"

"Where would you even get that kind of stuff?" I said, my stomach turning over.

"Angelo's—you know, the pawnshop. There's bound to be some jewelry there."

He scooched closer to the desk where I was sitting. "Let's get cracking on the plans. I've got to do it tonight."

"*Tonight?!*" He was getting crazier with each passing second. I had to stop this, or at least slow him down. "No way, dude. I have to think things through, look at every angle, double-check the store."

Jax scoffed. "Come on, Chris. You've been doing all that

for the past couple years for your comics. You know the layout of most of the local stores, their alarm systems, and a dozen different ways that Master Thief could break in."

"That's for my comics," I said. "If something goes wrong in my comics I can make up crap so it works out. Give the cops a flat tire. Create a jamming device that doesn't really exist. If something goes wrong tonight, you'll end up in prison."

"I'll be fine. Just give me the plan."

I leaned back in the desk chair and closed my eyes. This was too real. The thing with my comics is that I'd never actually finished one. I had lots of half-written stories and drawings, but because I hadn't fully thought through Master Thief, I couldn't figure out how to end anything. The comics always stopped after a successful heist. But then what happened?

I tried to picture what would happen tonight. Even if Jax broke into Angelo's and stole whatever he needed to pay off Fauxhawk, how would he make everything better with everyone else? With Mom and Dad? With the store's owners? With the police?

With me?

What if the story ended with Jax getting caught? Wouldn't it be my fault?

Then I started to think of something else. Where had Jax been when he was supposed to be at Stanford? What had he been doing all that time? Was it illegal—is that why he didn't want to tell us? Why wait this long to come home and tell us? Why did he bet so much money on my team when he knew we didn't have much of a chance to win? Was he that far gone as a gambling addict? Or was he hiding some other secret?

Either way, he needed to succeed tonight. And he couldn't do that alone.

"I'm going with you," I said.

He sat up so quickly that the pain in his ribs contorted his face. "No! That's out of the question!"

"You're injured."

"You're not going, bro. That's final. I'm still your older brother, and what I say goes."

# MY LIFE OF CRIME, PART TWO

**LOCK-PICKING** is not easy, even with the help of YouTube. You need to practice with a tension wrench and a hook pick until you get just the right feel to manipulate the tumblers, like I sometimes did on our front door lock when Mom and Dad weren't home. It's not as easy as it looks on cop shows when someone uses a bent fork to enter the Pentagon. It took four months before I was finally able to open the door without using my key. For me, it was just research for Master Thief. I never thought I'd do it for real. Yet here I was, in the dark, smelly, wet alley behind a strip mall, at three in the morning, scratching at the door to the Carpet and Flooring Emporium ("The Karpet Kings of OC!").

I had my hood up and cinched around my face, the same way I'd worn it a couple hours ago at the horror film. When I was sitting with Dad in the theater, my hood had been like Linus's security blanket. It represented my bond with my father and everything he'd ever taught me. Now, kneeling in front of this door, my hood was a disguise against security cameras, which went against everything

Dad had ever taught me. I had felt like a fraud when I was with Dad, and now I felt like a fraud with Jax. It was like I had a secret identity. But which was was the real me?

"Hurry up, SP," Jax said. He was keeping watch on the alley. One hand gripped a sledgehammer, and the other held a rusty crowbar, which we'd taken from the garage. Not that Dad ever used those tools. In fact, I think he'd borrowed the sledgehammer from neighbors that had moved away a couple years ago. The hard part was hiding them under our hoodies and lugging them from the car, which we'd parked several blocks away to avoid suspicion.

I kept working the lock, a task that was made harder by the thick orange rubber gloves I was wearing. They were all I could find around the house on short notice. The good news was that the package had never been opened, and I knew Mom wouldn't miss them. (One Sunday, she'd stared at the toilet with the gloves in one hand and a scrub brush in the other and said, "I don't think so." The next day she'd hired a weekly cleaning service.)

"Maybe we should try a window," Jax suggested impatiently.

"The windows are wired."

He sighed and bounced on his toes, nervously looking up and down the alley. Sometimes he looked overhead, as if expecting to see helicopters.

"I thought you said you've done this before," he complained.

"You wanna try?" I said.

That shut him up.

"Got it," I said, my voice cracking with relief. Let me tell you, picking a lock wired to an alarm is not the same as picking the lock to your front door while stopping occasionally for Gatorade and pretzels.

We both hurried inside and closed the door behind us. Adrenaline was pumping through my system as if someone had stuck a hose in my mouth and turned on the spigot. I took a few seconds to allow my body to stop vibrating and to remind myself to breathe.

"You okay?" Jax asked.

"Fine," I said, but the word came out like a bird chirp, as if the sound could barely squeeze out of my constricted throat.

I looked over at the GE Simon XT security box on the wall. The blue screen gave the time (3:07 A.M.) and the security status (ARMED). If we had forced the door open, the alarms would have been blaring.

I walked through the back room out to the storefront, where all the wood-flooring and carpet samples were arranged in bright displays. This is where people picked what "look" they wanted, but the actual wood and carpets were stored somewhere else in some warehouse. The whole storefront room was about the size of our living room.

Jax looked around, confused. "Chris, why are we in here? We're supposed to be hitting Angelo's, remember?"

"A place like Angelo's, with thousands of dollars' worth of merchandise, is going to have a pretty elaborate security system. Something I wouldn't have a clue about bypassing. But a place like this doesn't need much security—just enough to discourage vandals. They don't have anything here worth stealing."

"Hate to point out the obvious, but the goal of this mission isn't just to break into anyplace, it's to break into a place *with stuff valuable enough to take so I don't get another beating—or worse.*"

I went to the wall and shoved aside a display rack of flooring samples. I knocked lightly on the wall. When I found the stud, I marked the wall with an *X*.

"Checking for termites?" he scoffed.

"This store is only a year old. So is the store next door. Both of these stores used to be one bigger store."

"I remember," Jax said. "A video store."

"Yup. Now that everyone downloads their films or rents them online, no more Blockbuster. So they divided that big store into two smaller stores. This place and—"

"And Angelo's," Jax interrupted, smiling.

I nodded. I knocked again on the wall until I found the other stud and marked it with an *X*. "Sixteen inches apart. Plenty of room for us to squeeze through. We can break through the wall here and we'll get inside the pawnshop without setting off their alarms."

"What about motion sensors?"

"Doesn't need them. The doors and windows are not only wired, but he has metal gates over them. He also has a couple other measures inside."

"How do you know all this?" he asked, impressed.

"I had a story line in one of my comics where Master Thief has to steal a guitar with a safety-deposit-box key hidden inside it. I cased Angelo's to make my story more realistic, and I figured out exactly how he'd steal the guitar."

He grinned. "Best brother *ever.*"

We both went to work busting the drywall with the sledgehammer and crowbar. Ten minutes later we were standing in the pawnshop. Video cameras were mounted in each corner, but they were on standby.

Jax rushed over to one of the display cases filled with jewelry. Three black metal earring trees sat on the display case at one-foot intervals. Each had a couple pairs of sparkly earrings dangling from the metal branches. Jax reached for one of the pairs.

"No!" I croaked in a whisper-shout.

He lowered his hand. "What the heck, Chris! This is no time to back out."

"I'm not backing out. I'm just trying to keep you from setting off the alarm and activating the security cameras." I pointed to the jewelry trees. "Those earrings are just imitations. They're meant to get you to grab them first, because they're out in the open. Once you touch them, you move the tree, which activates the alarm and the security cameras, which are positioned to get what's called a 'prosecutable image.'"

"So how are we supposed to get the jewelry? I could smash the front of the case while you hold the jewelry stands." He raised his sledgehammer over his shoulder.

"That won't work either," I said. "The inside of the case is wired so that if the glass breaks, it triggers the alarm."

"Great!" He lowered the sledgehammer. "So, what's the plan?"

I pointed at the far corner. "Bring me one of those vacuum cleaners. The Dyson DC41."

He gave me a strange look. "You know the make and brand of vacuum cleaners?"

"Part of the job, dude. As legendary UCLA coach John Wooden said, 'Failure to prepare is preparing to fail.'"

Jax shrugged and retrieved the vacuum cleaner. "Holy crap, this thing is selling for three hundred bucks."

I took it from him and placed it next to me while I knelt in front of the display case. "They retail for six hundred and seventy dollars, so that's a real bargain."

He chuckled. "Again, bro, it's scary that you know that."

"Just plug it in," I said. He did. "And pull down your ski mask, just in case this doesn't work." He pulled ski mask over his face. I did the same, then pulled my hood on top of that.

I dug into my backpack and removed the Silverline circle glass cutter I had found on eBay. I fastened the suction cup to the front of the display case. It works just like a compass you use to draw circles, only instead of a pencil on the moving arm, there's a glass cutter. I cut a four-inch circle into the case, popped out the glass, and stuck the Dyson hose through the opening. I started the vacuum, and its 235 air watts began sucking up every earring, bracelet, necklace, brooch, and watch in the case. They all went into a purple plastic bin with a .55-gallon capacity. (See how much detail you have to know to be Master Thief?) In less than two minutes, we had thousands of dollars' worth of merchandise. I removed the bin from the vacuum and emptied the jewelry into my backpack.

"Let's go," I said.

Jax stood there a moment, staring at me. Suddenly he pulled up his mask to show me a big smile of awe and respect. "Dude, you did it! That was all so clever. Breaking in next door, using the glass cutter and the vacuum. Man, you *are* Master Thief!"

"Yeah, maybe we can celebrate when we get home." He couldn't see my face, but under the mask I was grinning a little at his praise. Plus, I was shocked that my plan had worked. Just like I'd written it in my comics. "Now put your mask on and let's go."

We started for the hole in the wall to make our escape back through the carpet store.

"Chris, I'm so grateful, dude," Jax said. He was reaching to pull his mask back down as he followed me toward the hole. "You really—"

Then everything went wrong.

Starting with the alarm.

# PRESENT

# COPS "R" US

**"WHY** do you think Officer Crane brought you to my office?" Principal McDonald asked. His sharpened pencil hovered over his notepad, ready to etch my every word into a permanent record that would follow me throughout my entire life. Especially to Stanford.

*Ever arrested, kid? Any criminal record?*

"Yeah," Officer Crane said. "Why did I bring you here?"

"I don't know," I answered. "There have been a lot of garage break-ins. Are you questioning everybody in school to find out if they've seen anything?"

Officer Crane sneered.

Principal McDonald said nothing. He just stared at me, tapping his pencil eraser on the blank paper like a metronome.

This is a classic technique, kids. Every authority figure from a cop to a parent to a teacher uses it to break his victim. Few people can endure prolonged silence without feeling an internal itch that is only satisfied by vomiting up a bunch of words. Silence seems to grow in a room until it squeezes out all the air and leaves the poor victim gasping for breath.

But that wouldn't work on me. Silence and I went way back.

To fill the time, I imagined Principal McDonald's pad of paper to be a ravenous wolf anxious to be fed with my words. The tapping eraser was just teasing it, poking the wild animal into a slathering frenzy. It was growling for words, snapping at the air in front of our mouths. But I wouldn't feed the rabid beast. I'd starve it with my silence.

Maybe there was a comic book villain in there somewhere.

The silence stretched like Mr. Fantastic's elastic body.

Officer Crane coughed. He shifted nervously. He was starting to sweat.

Principal McDonald ignored him, keeping his icy gaze on me.

I read his T-shirt again:

"THE ONLY THING NECESSARY FOR THE TRIUMPH OF EVIL IS FOR GOOD MEN TO DO NOTHING."
EDMUND BURKE

I was good at doing nothing and saying nothing. Did that mean I was responsible for all the evil in the world?

Last night I had done a lot. I'd picked a lock, broken through a wall, and robbed a pawnshop of almost fifteen thousand dollars' worth of jewelry.

Not to mention what I did to the cops. I guess you could call all that evil.

"There was a robbery last night, Richards," Officer Crane finally blurted. I'd predicted that he'd be the first to crack.

"Another garage?" I asked innocently.

Principal McDonald laughed. "Oh boy, Chris. You are really entertaining me today. More surprises than I've had in the last five years. And that includes last year when Mr. Cooper, in front of his horrified and delighted drama class, bent over to pick up a script from the floor, ripped the seat of his pants from stem to stern, and had to rush home to change."

"Yeah," I said. "That was funny."

Principal McDonald stared at me again, his leathery face grim with accusation. His beard looked like the prow of a ship ready to ram me.

That got to me. After all, I liked him. He was a cool guy who really cared about us. When the band couldn't raise enough money through their car wash to go to some regional competition, he kicked in eight hundred dollars of his own money. He'd never bragged about it either. I only found out because my dad had kicked in the final two hundred bucks himself, even though I wasn't even in band.

I looked down in embarrassment, thinking about how good Principal McDonald and my dad were. And what a criminal I was.

"Talk to us, Chris," Principal McDonald said softly. He rubbed his eyes wearily, as if all this accusing was taking a toll on him.

I looked up at him, not sure what to do. I could remain silent, no problem. But just the thought of telling him everything made me feel like I'd be shrugging off a five-hundred-pound backpack that had me hunched over and crawling on my knees. I'd be able to walk again. Feel light. Breathe.

Then again, if I told him, lives would be destroyed. And I'd be betraying my brother. That had to be some major evil, too.

I stared at him, remembering everything that had happened last night. Especially the part after Jax had tripped the alarm.

I still don't know how it happened. Jax and I were heading toward the hole in the wall and a clean getaway when he somehow bumped into the display case. I looked back just in time to see one of the jewelry trees topple over and clatter on top of the glass counter. Instantly, lights started flashing, an alarm started blaring, and the security cameras clicked on, the red lights turning green. I yanked Jax's ski mask down, but I didn't know if I was too late.

Did they now have a "prosecutable image" of his face?

We scampered through the hole out the back door of the carpet store. The whole time I was wondering how Jax, the most athletic person I'd ever met, could bump into a wired display case. Was he drunk? On drugs?

Or was I right about his secret? His real secret.

Too much was going on for me to figure it out right then.

By the time we were running down the alley, we heard the sirens of two police cars heading our way. Jax grabbed me by the arm and yanked me backward into the shadows. We crouched behind a Dumpster overflowing with cardboard boxes.

A cop car screeched in from the opposite end of the alley. Another appeared in ahead of us and pulled up next to the other one. They parked, each pointing in the opposite direction.

I know what you're thinking: we should jump into the Dumpster, burrow down to the bottom, and wait until the police cars leave. Cops have seen the same movies as you, so it was just a matter of time before they began searching each Dumpster.

So, we waited.

Two cops jumped out of each car. The four of them discussed their plan of action for about twenty seconds. Then two cops removed their guns and flashlights and headed into the carpet store. The other two ran in opposite directions down the alley in search of us.

My planning hadn't taken into account being trapped behind a Dumpster with armed cops chasing after us. In my comic book, Master Thief got away before the cops arrived. But then, he didn't have a brother setting off alarms and getting his picture taken.

The back of the alley was lined with an eight-foot chain-link fence. On the other side of the fence were a stand of trees and a mobile home park. At least there wasn't any razor wire on top of the fence.

"Let's make a run for it," I said. "We can climb the fence and get away through the park."

Yeah, desperate, but it's all I could come up with.

I started to get up to run, but Jax held me back. "They'll hear us," he said.

"Not with those alarms blaring."

Just then the alarms went silent. Perfect.

"The cops know that if we got out of this alley, we're long gone," Jax whispered. "So they are only going to run to the end of the alley. Then they'll turn around and come back, searching every nook and cranny and Dumpster on the way back."

"What do we do?" I said. I heard the panic in my voice. I hoped he didn't.

"Follow me. Now!" Suddenly Jax bolted across the alley and I blindly followed, just like I'd blindly followed his robbery idea. When was I going to learn?

Once we reached the other side, I looked to my left and right. The two cops were nearly to the end of the alley. In a few more feet, they would turn around and see us illuminated by the lights.

"Let's wait outside," one of the cops from inside the carpet shop said.

"Good idea," the other cop said. "My ears are still ringing from that alarm."

Great. Now they were coming out, too.

Oh, by the way, what was Jax doing running *toward* the patrol cars??

When Jax got to the back of the police car near the fence, he grabbed the rear bumper and slid under the car.

Naturally, I did the same.

We lay underneath, side by side.

*Now what?* I mouthed.

He removed his cell phone and punched in 911. "Hello?" he whispered into the phone. "I just saw two men running through my mobile park. Oh my God, there they are now. Help us!" He clicked off just as the two cops came out of the store.

The cops started yelling to each other, asking if they'd found anything.

"They can trace that call to your phone," I whispered while they yelled.

"Not this phone," he said.

I looked at him. Since when did he have the kind of throwaway phone favored by criminals? (Master Thief had one, of course. More than one.) How did this information fit into my guess about his secret?

For days I'd been gathering stray bits of information,

inconsistencies in what certain people had said and done, and I'd started to formulate a theory about why Jax had been lying.

The radio in one of the patrol cars crackled to life. It was hard to hear what it was saying, but I heard "two male suspects" and "mobile home park."

"Jim! Travis!" one of the cops called to the other two searching the alley. "They're running through the mobile home park next door."

"Mobile home park?" one of the cops from the store said with a chuckle. "Who lives in a mobile home park anymore?"

"My cousin, for one," the other cop said, with an edge to his voice.

"Well, maybe a tornado will pop up and carry them away. Isn't that what happens in these places?"

"Just for that, I'm gonna kick your butt at racquetball tomorrow."

"Only if you wake up in Oz and Glinda grants you a wish."

They both laughed at that.

These cops certainly didn't seem like they were on high alert.

Jim and Travis jogged up to the other two. The cop with the mobile home cousin started giving orders. He told Jim and Travis to take one car, and the racquetball cop to take the other. One would patrol the perimeter of the mobile home park and the other would drive through it, trying to flush the perps out. (It felt weird to be called a *perp*.) Meanwhile, Boss Cop would wait inside the shop for Angelo to arrive.

Boss Cop walked toward the building as the others jumped into their patrol cars and started the engines. Jax pulled me close to him so that we were both away from the tires. The cars pulled away in opposite directions and we lay in the alley holding our breath as the Boss Cop kept walking toward the carpet-store back door. If he turned around, he'd see us lying there like worms and it would be game over.

But he didn't turn around.

Half an hour later we made it to Jax's car, which he'd parked in an all-night supermarket parking lot a couple miles away. On the fifteen-minute drive home, we didn't talk about what had just happened.

Instead, I asked him, "Why did you set up another basketball game with the Undertakers?"

"Relax, Kobe. There's no pressure to win. I just needed a place in the open where I could give him the jewelry. Last time I met him alone, he rearranged my rib cage."

"You could do it in a mall."

"I suggested that, but he refused. Said no one pays attention to what adults are doing when a bunch of kids are playing nearby."

"Those guys are animals," I said.

"It's just for show, bro. Play it safe, let them win, no one gets hurt. Rand gets the jewels, I get rid of my debt, everyone's a winner. Right?"

I didn't answer.

"Right?" he repeated. "I mean it, Chris, don't try to make a game of it, or someone could get hurt."

"Right," I said. But I didn't look at him or speak the rest of the way home.

I couldn't sleep for the two hours left before I had to get up for school. I just kept going over everything that had happened during the past few days since Jax had returned home. I kept trying to focus on the little clues here and there that told me there was something else going on with him, something he wasn't telling us. But my mind kept coming back to one thing:

*We'd actually gotten away with it.*

"Just tell us what happened, Chris," Principal McDonald asked again.

I looked at his kind face for a full minute before answering. "I don't know what you're talking about."

Principal McDonald sighed, clearly disappointed.

Officer Crane bent over and stuck his face so close to mine that I could have bitten his nose without much effort. "Listen to me, you little brat, we have a photograph of your brother robbing Angelo's Pawnshop. And he wasn't alone. *Now* do you know what I'm talking about?"

I tried to look confused. "I'm sorry, Officer, but are you arresting me? If so, you need to read me my Miranda rights. Perhaps I should talk to my parents."

"No one's being arrested," Principal McDonald said.

"Maybe. Maybe not." Officer Crane stood up straight so he could tower menacingly over me. "California law states that I have the right to question a minor without parental consent or presence."

"Knock it off, both of you," Principal McDonald said, irritated.

"Yes, sir," I said. "But I think Officer Crane needs to be informed that minors can only be questioned by police if they *agree* to be questioned. The U.S. Supreme Court implied that schools create a 'custodial' situation, which means you're supposed to inform me that I have the right to leave at any time without answering any questions."

Officer Crane's face was the same shade of red as a baboon's butt.

"Look it up, if you don't believe me," I continued. "The case is *J.D.B. v. North Carolina*. It involves a thirteen-year-old who was interrogated in school for burglary."

Part of my time lying awake this morning had been spent Googling law cases in preparation for this possibility.

"You don't seem surprised about the photo of Jax," Principal McDonald said.

I stood up and headed for the door. "I'm not surprised, because I know it wasn't him." I opened the door. "Now,

I've got English class and I'm already ten minutes late."

Officer Crane shook an angry fist at me. "You punk kid, you're going to—"

I closed the door behind me and hurried off to class. I might have sounded all brave in there, but my hands were shaking so much that I stopped in the boys' bathroom to splash water on my face. Then I dialed Jax's phone—his regular phone, not the burner he'd had last night. He didn't pick up and I didn't want to leave anything incriminating, so I just said, "The police questioned me about some burglary at a pawnshop last night. Wanted to ask me about some photo. Weird, huh?"

Hopefully, that would let him know to stay hidden until he'd finished whatever he was plotting regarding Fauxhawk. I was pretty sure I was close to figuring out exactly what that was.

# DO YOU KNOW WHAT COLOR YOUR ORANGE IS?

**"WHAT** color is an orange?" Mr. Laubaugh asked the class as I entered the room. He looked over at me and smiled as if nothing in the world had changed. As if I hadn't burglarized a pawnshop, hidden under a patrol car, and been interrogated in the principal's office by a cop whose breath stank of stale coffee and wet dog fur.

"Come in, Chris. Maybe you can answer the question that seems to have stumped the rest of the class."

I took my seat, glancing across the room at Brooke. Her attention was focused on Mr. Laubaugh. She didn't even look my way. Not even the usual dismissive glare. More unusual, her hand wasn't waving in the air, demanding to answer the question.

However, the rest of the class was looking at me. Word had already gotten around about me being hauled out of algebra by Officer Crane. By now the whole school knew.

"We're not stumped, Mr. L," said Theo. "We're waiting for you to explain the question."

"What's to explain? The question is the model of simplicity: what color is an orange?"

"Nothing's simple with you," Theo said. "You've always got some crazy twist on things."

"Maybe this time is different," Mr. Laubaugh said with a grin that confirmed this time was not any different.

"Chris," Dave Jaspers whispered to me, "what happened with the cop? Did you see a crime or something?"

"Was someone murdered?" Char Gleeson asked, a little too gleefully.

I mouthed *Later* and turned back in my seat to face Mr. Laubaugh.

"And to motivate you, here's today's prize." Mr. Laubaugh held up a battered DVD case of a movie I'd never heard of called *The 400 Blows*. The cover was a black-and-white photo of a frowning boy with his face pressed up against a chain-link fence, like he was in prison.

"Why is the cover in black and white?" asked Kevin Yee, our movie expert (as long as the movie had a lot of explosions and aliens).

"Because the film is in black and white," answered Mr. Laubaugh.

The class groaned as if he'd just told them he was giving them a surprise test on everything they'd ever learned since kindergarten.

"That's not all," Mr. Laubaugh said. "The film is in French. With subtitles."

The class's groan was even louder, like zombies just noticing a helpless toddler.

"French. Subtitles. That's not really motivating us to

answer the question," Dave Jaspers said. "Might as well tell us you're giving us a healthy tofu snack."

"Hey," Karen Flannigan protested. "Tofu is awesome. And doesn't kill animals."

A couple other vegans nodded approval, but everyone else ignored her.

"How come you know so many movies and books and TV shows that no one's ever heard of?" Clancy Timmons called from the back of the room.

"Actually, a lot of people have heard of this film. It's won many prestigious awards and was even nominated for an Oscar. It's considered one of the best films ever made."

"What's it about?" Theo asked.

"A twelve-year-old boy growing up in Paris in the early 1950s who's misunderstood by his parents and teachers and gets thrown in jail for the night."

Did Mr. Laubaugh just look right at me? Did he know something about last night?

"If it's so great, how come I haven't heard of it?" Clancy said defiantly, as if Mr. Laubaugh was personally challenging his intelligence.

"'There are more things in heaven and earth,' Clancy, 'than are dreamt of in your philosophy.'"

*"Hamlet!"* most of the class said in unison. Mr. Laubaugh had spent a whole class on the meaning of that single quote at the beginning of the semester. *If you understand* Hamlet, he'd told us, *you understand all of life.*

I still didn't understand *Hamlet*. Maybe that's why life was kicking my butt.

Mr. Laubaugh nodded. "Tell you what, Clancy. I'm going to let you use your cell phone to look up the movie on Rotten Tomatoes. Tell me what the rating is."

Clancy took out his phone and tapped it a few times. As he read, his face looked shocked. "It has a one hundred percent Fresh rating. I've never seen that high a rating before."

"More things in heaven and earth, Clancy." Mr. Laubaugh smiled and waggled the DVD. "Now, who can tell me what color is an orange?"

"Orange?" Cole Tish said.

Everyone laughed.

"Someone had to say it!" Cole said defensively.

"You're partially right, Cole," Mr. Laubaugh said. "In the U.S., oranges grown in early spring or late fall are orange. But those grown the rest of the year aren't. And oranges grown in South America and other countries near the equator are *never* orange on the outside."

"Wait," Jeff Blanco said. "Isn't that where we get the name for the color orange? From the fruit?"

"No," said Theo. "The use of orange to describe the color occurred three hundred years after the fruit first showed up in Europe. The fruit got its name from the Sanskrit word for fragrant: *naranja*. Which sounds kinda like orange."

The class stared at Theo like he'd just barfed up a Volkswagen.

"How do you even know that, dude?" Clancy said.

"Some kid from Roosevelt mentioned it during an Aca-lympics contest. It just stuck in my head. Sounds like a magic spell. *Naranja!*" He made a conjuring gesture with his hands. A girl chuckled and Theo lowered his hands, embarrassed.

I looked over at Brooke again. Usually when Theo, or anyone else, offered some chicken nugget of obscure information, she would snort or glare or wave her hand to argue the point. Today she just sat quietly at her desk. A model student.

"Mr. Laubaugh," Cole said, "I don't see what any of this has to do with *The Catcher in the Rye*. Is this stuff going to be on the test?"

"I'll get to that in a minute. But first, anyone want to answer the original question? What color is an orange?"

If you were expecting me to answer, get used to disappointment. I had no idea.

"Yellow?" Cole guessed.

Mr. Laubaugh shook his head and waited for someone else to answer.

"Green," Brooke finally said. Usually, she answered every question defiantly, like the snapping of a wet towel against a bare thigh. This time her voice was softer. "Ripe oranges are green in most of the world. Once they start turning orange they're actually rotting. They're green because of all the chlorophyll and only turn orange when exposed to cold. Because most Americans think that a green fruit means it's not ripe, the farmers sometimes expose the oranges to ethylene gas, which knocks out the chlorophyll. Some places blast them with cold or even dye the skin orange so people will buy them."

"Ewww," a few students said.

"Excellent answer, Brooke," Mr. Laubaugh said. He walked over to her and handed her the DVD. "For your growing collection," he said, acknowledging that she'd won more DVDs than anyone else in class.

"I still don't get the point," Cole said, clearly frustrated. "I mean, why bring it up in English class instead of science class?"

"You can't tell an orange by its cover?" Dave Jaspers asked. "Like a book?"

A few students chuckled.

Mr. Laubaugh grinned. "Not bad, Dave. Not bad. But maybe I have something more subtle in mind. Something that relates to the literary themes we've discussed all year. What do all the works we've read have in common? What is the main mistake that the fictional characters often make, including our friend Holden Caulfield?"

Everyone concentrated on coming up with an answer. Sure, we had some smart-asses in the class, but this was an advanced class and you didn't get in here by not caring. Theo was tugging on his lower lip, the way he always did when he was thinking. Clancy puffed out his cheeks like he was about to dive into the deep end of the pool. Brooke squinted, as if she was trying to read the answer through the wall.

Suddenly I was talking, the words tumbling out before I realized it was me speaking them. "The characters are like the orange. They keep trying to be what others want them to be. Even if it means getting gassed, frozen, or dyed. Even if it kills something inside, like the chlorophyll. All that wasted effort and pain to be what others think they want. Like Kermit says, 'It's not easy being green.'"

The class just stared for a long minute, as if I'd just recited the Greek alphabet.

Even Mr. Laubaugh seemed shocked. Then a huge smile spread across his face and he said, "Now *that's* what I'm talking about!"

# SOMETHING TO SHOW YOU

**OUTSIDE** the classroom I pulled Theo aside. "I need your help," I said.

"Not until you tell me what went on with Officer Crane."

"You know him?"

"My dad works with him. Says he's kind of a tool."

"Your dad's right." Other kids going by glanced at me and whispered, still wondering why the police had hauled me out of class. "It was no big deal. They just wanted to know about my brother."

Theo shook his head. "Man, what has Jax gotten himself into?"

"That's what I'm trying to find out. And I need your help with the research, because I don't have the time to do it."

"Again? What's in it for me?" he asked. He saw my surprised expression and gave me a light punch to the arm. "JK, man, JK. I'm just messing with you."

I told him what I needed: a list of the families who'd been victims of garage break-ins, from the police log.

He looked excited. "You're onto something, aren't you?"

"I don't know. I've just been trying to look for patterns, the way we do with the stories in Mr. Laubaugh's class."

"You mean like 'If you can understand *Hamlet*, you can understand all of life'?"

"Did you understand *Hamlet*?"

Theo shrugged. "To me it was about a dude torn between doing what his ghost dad wants him to do and what he thinks he should do."

Was that life? To always be torn between two choices, never sure which is the right one? How old did you have to be before that went away?

"Who would you go with?" Theo asked.

"I don't know. Personally, I don't think any good can come from listening to a ghost."

"Me neither. Although in one of the Pirates of the Caribbean movies the guy's dad was a part of that ghost ship. Remember that scene where he just peeled away from the hull? Yuck."

I didn't say anything to that.

Theo changed topics. "Dude, you gotta let me in on this garage thing. I've got a reputation to uphold as a detective, you know. Does it have something to do with Officer Crane questioning you?"

"Text me the info as soon as you can, and I'll tell you everything."

"I'm on the case," Theo said, and took off. He was so tall that it looked like his head was a balloon floating above the rest of the students on their way to the cafeteria.

I hurried down the hall toward my locker. It was lunch and I wanted to use this time to talk to everyone about playing the Undertakers after school.

Just as I'd shoved my backpack into the locker, I felt a tug on my shirt. When I turned around, Brooke was standing there. She handed me a folded piece of paper. I looked at it. An address.

"Come to my house at six. We'll watch Mr. Laubaugh's stupid French movie."

I was too surprised to say anything.

"This whole Strong, Silent Cowboy doesn't really work for me, you know."

"It doesn't work for me either," I said.

She laughed. "See? You're funny when you want to be."

I tried to think of something funny to say. Couldn't. Not so funny after all.

"What did the cops want? Did you continue your shop-lifting spree after you left yesterday?" Her voice was joking, but her eyes looked concerned.

I shook my head. "It's nothing. Just wanted to know about my brother."

"Is he in trouble?"

"Nope."

She stared at me like she was X-raying my skull, probing my brain for the truth.

"Why were you so quiet in class?" I asked her, to break her stare.

"Quiet? Did you not notice my brilliant lecture on green oranges?"

"Yes, brilliant. But you weren't your usual Cruella self. Not one sarcastic snort."

She shrugged. "I dunno. Maybe it was hanging out with you yesterday. Some of that quietude rubbed off."

This time I laughed. "*You* can be funny when you want to."

"So, you coming over?" she asked.

"I'll have to ask my parents."

"You'll figure a way." She started to walk away. "There's something I want to show you."

"What?" I called after her.

She didn't turn around. "You'll see tonight. If your parents let you."

She snorted sarcastically.

# BLINDFOLD BASKETBALL

**"YOU** boys wearing blindfolds don't move until I call your name," Coach Mandrake said.

Yeah, you heard right. Blindfolds!

"When I do call your name, slowly walk straight forward. And I mean *walk*, don't run. I don't want anyone getting hurt."

I was one of the kids wearing a blindfold. One of the guys he didn't want getting hurt. That was my sentiment, too.

"Coach, have you been watching Bruce Lee movies again?" Juvy asked. I couldn't see him, but he was standing somewhere to the left of me.

"Yeah," Sami said. "You're getting all Zen kung-fu-y on us."

A few boys chuckled.

Coach scoffed. "This is a little drill I designed to help you guys pass the ball better. Last couple games there were a lot of bad passes that caused unforced turnovers. Weston, no more behind-the-back passes. Most of them go out-of-bounds anyway."

"But I look so cool as they do, Coach," Weston joked.

I could tell by the silence that Coach was giving Weston the Frozen Stare. Those on the receiving end usually just stood perfectly still, afraid to move. Even jokester Weston knew better than to wisecrack during the Frozen Stare.

Coach continued: "Sami, use a bounce pass on the pick-and-roll unless you have a clear opening for a bullet pass. Thomas, don't just toss the ball in the general vicinity of the player, pass it right to his chest. That way he can drive or shoot. If he has to chase it or bend down for it, the defense has time to get into position. Got it?"

"Got it," we all said.

"GOT IT?" Coach shouted.

"GOT IT!" we shouted back.

"Here's what's going to happen. When I call your name, one of you boys in the blindfolded line will walk forward, dribbling the ball. On either side of you, scattered around the court, will be your teammates. One of them will shout 'Ball!' and you will immediately pass the ball to them. Got it?"

"I don't got it, Coach," Roger said. He was standing in front of me, also blindfolded. We were the only two in the blindfolded line. "I'm just supposed to guess where the player is?"

"Not guess. Listen. When you hear his voice, imagine where on the court he's standing, and fire a chest pass to him. GOT IT?"

"So, like Marco Polo, but with a ball," Sami said.

Coach's sigh was as loud as a steam locomotive. "Yes, Sami. Like Marco Polo. GOT IT?"

"GOT IT!" we responded.

"Roger, go!" Coach said.

I could hear Roger slowly dribbling as he walked forward. Suddenly from the left, Juvy hollered, "Ball!"

Roger hesitated.

"Pass the ball!" Coach said.

The next things I heard were a ball bouncing away and everyone laughing.

"Better get your hearing checked," Juvy said. "That missed me by about five feet."

"Not bad for your first time, Roger," Coach said. "Let's see how the rest of you do before you start making fun of anyone."

My pass went two feet to the right of Three and a foot over his head.

Everyone messed up pretty badly their first time blindfolded, but after an hour, we were all getting the ball on target or very close.

"Hey, Coach," Weston said, "if you want to really make this interesting, we need to add a danger factor, like fire or razor blades."

We ended the practice with a scrimmage, and by then everyone was passing the ball with amazing speed and accuracy.

When practice was over, we were all pretty excited about our new skill. It got me thinking about how good it felt to pass the ball and trust that my teammate would be there to catch it. That's what I'd been doing my whole life with Jax, trusting that he'd be there, while he trusted that I would be there. Blind faith.

When we got into the locker room Roger buzzkilled the excitement when he said, "Man, I don't know about going up against those Undertaker dudes today."

"You told me at lunch that you would, Roger," I said, trying not to sound desperate. "Everyone else is playing."

"You can get someone else. Maybe Theo."

"I'll play," Juvy volunteered.

"I appreciate that, Juvy," I said, "but it's got to be the same team."

Roger shrugged. "The same team that got shoved around by those bigger, older kids? The ones who gave you a shiner and a busted nose?"

"Payback time!" Juvy piped in. He wasn't helping.

"It's good practice for high school," Tom said. "We're going to face a lot of bigger kids then. They're bringing them over from Africa and China. Seven-foot giants that will make it hard for us to get on a college team."

"I don't care," Roger said. "I'm never going to make a college team anyway." It was the first time he'd ever said that, even though it was probably true. His body was built more for football than basketball, except he loved basketball and only tolerated football.

"Probably none of us will play for a college team," I said. "But who cares? We're playing now and we love it now."

That was my Big Inspirational Locker Room Speech. No one looked inspired.

"We can beat them, Roger," I said. "We almost beat them yesterday."

"Until they broke your nose, dude."

"It wasn't broken. It was just . . . bloody." That sounded lame, even to me.

Roger didn't say anything. He just took his school clothes from his locker and started stuffing them into his backpack. That meant he wasn't changing, which meant he was going to the park to play with us.

"So," he said, slinging his backpack over one shoulder as we walked out, "what's up with the cops interrogating you today? I heard you'd murdered someone and ate their cat."

"Something like that," I said.

# REMATCH OF VENGEANCE!

**"I'VE** got a plan," I said.

Rain, Gee, Roger, and Tom looked skeptical.

"Seriously," I said.

Their expressions didn't change.

Before practice today I'd stopped in the coach's office for advice. "Coach, how do you beat a team that's bigger and stronger than you?"

"Are their skills just as good?" he'd asked.

I'd nodded.

"Easy answer. You don't beat them."

He'd been standing at his desk, rummaging through a mess of papers, looking for something. He returned to his rummaging. Conversation over.

"But underdogs win all the time," I'd continued. "How many times in the NBA have we seen one of the worst teams beat one of the best? And in tennis, guys ranked in the hundreds are always knocking off top seeds. And some nobody boxer knocks out the champ."

"Sure, Chris, it happens. But not often. That's why it makes news when it does happen."

"Okay, but how do you make that happen?"

Coach Mandrake stopped rummaging, looked at me, and tugged his goatee. "The rule of sports is simple: no matter how good you are, if there's somebody with the same skills but who's bigger, the bigger guy will almost always win."

"Almost always," I'd repeated. "How do you make the 'almost always' happen?"

He'd raked his fingers through the goatee like a farmer preparing the soil for planting. "Trickery," he'd said.

"Trickery?" Gee said when I told them about my meeting with Coach. "Is that even a word?"

"Like what?" Rain asked. "Did he offer anything specific?"

"Not really," I said. "But I came up with a few ideas that might give us an edge."

When I explained them, Roger slapped me on the back. "Dude, I never knew you were so devious."

I thought back to yesterday with Brooke. *You're a lot more devious than I would have expected, Chris Richards.* And that was before my night of crime.

I just nodded. If they only knew.

Fifteen minutes later Rand (a.k.a. Fauxhawk) and the Gold Coasters (a.k.a. Undertakers) arrived. Predictably, Fauxhawk had his hair spiked straight up into a frozen blond wave. He wore a black hoodie with a big *A* on the chest like Superman's *S*. The *A* was outlined in blue with red in the middle. I could think of at least one R-rated word the *A* might stand for in his case.

"Hey, kid!" Fauxhawk barked as he approached the court. "Where the hell's your retarded brother?"

I shrugged. What was it about that *A* on his chest that kept nagging at me?

He looked around the park, then back to the parking lot. His focus was on Jax showing up with the goods, not on the game. Especially since there was no bet. To him, the game was only a cover for their exchange.

But *we* were playing to win. I figured the Undertakers felt the same way.

"How's the nose, kid?" Masterson asked with a smirk. "Mommy kiss and make it better?"

"You going to forfeit again?" Danforth asked. "Why not do it now and save your friends the humiliation?"

I said nothing, so he shrugged and hurried off with his team to stretch.

They looked even bigger today.

Fauxhawk didn't bother huddling with his team or giving them any coaching advice. He paced on the sidelines, looking around nervously.

The rest of my team was on the court warming up their shots. I just stood there studying the *A* on his hoodie, trying to dig through my brain to uncover the voice that was trying to tell me something. Before I could find the voice, my cell phone buzzed. I went over to the grass and pulled it from my hoodie pocket.

"I got the info you wanted," Theo said. "It was all public

record, so it wasn't much of a challenge." He sounded disappointed.

"How old are the children in each of the victim families?"

I could hear the rusting of paper as he looked through the documents.

"Varies," he said. "They've got kids of all ages."

"Right; what I meant was, do they all have children under the age of ten?"

More rustling. "Yes! How'd you know?"

"I think I figured out how the garage robberies are done. And who's been doing them."

"Tell me!" he said excitedly.

"Later," I said. "I need one more thing from you."

"Dude, I'm not your sidekick. Need I remind you that I'm a detective, too?"

"I know, I know. You're the guy who inspired me to figure it out. Besides, I'm not really a detective. I just stumbled on this whole mess while trying to figure out what was going on with my brother."

Theo sighed. "Okay, last favor."

I told him what I needed.

"That's a lot of phone calls, Chris."

"Use your charm," I said.

He laughed. "It'll take me an hour. If I use my charm, it'll take two hours."

"Cancel that order of charm," I said.

He said he'd text me the results.

"Thanks, man, I really appreciate it." I hung up feeling a little guilty that I couldn't tell Theo everything I'd figured out. About Jax's real story. About the garage burglaries. About everything. Not yet. Not until I was certain.

I tapped in Jax's number and sent him a text: *I know everything.*

I waited. No response.

Maybe I was wrong. Maybe everything I thought I'd figured out was the equivalent of a three-point air ball.

I texted again: *Wait until after our game.*

Again, I waited. Again, no response.

"Dude," Roger called. "You gonna warm up, or what?"

"Be right there," I said.

I stared at my phone. Come on, Jax. *I know you got my texts. I know you know what I meant.* Right?

I was about to text again when Jax finally answered: *You have 15 mins.*

"Let's get this over with," Masterson said, leading his team onto the court. "I've got more important things to do with my life than step on ants all day."

A couple of his teammates chuckled.

We didn't respond. We weren't there to trade insults; we were there to beat them. Right now I had to forget about Jax and Fauxhawk and Stanford and Brooke and my parents and the police and what everyone expected from me.

Right now, I just wanted to win.

# REVENGE BALL

**FOR** some reason, as I walked onto the court, I thought, What color is an orange? If you asked an orange, it would probably say, "Who cares?" It's like asking me what is my passion? I have lots of passions: basketball, comics, Mr. L's class. Why do I have to put a name to it, call it a color?

"Shoot for outs?" I challenged Masterson, tossing him the ball.

He dribbled it a couple times. "Kinda bouncy," he said.

It was. We'd deliberately pumped it up before they got here so it was a little overinflated. An inflated ball would bounce farther away from the rim in a missed shot, neutralizing the height advantage the Undertakers had under the basket. While they were crashing the boards for rebounds, missed shots would be bouncing back into our hands.

He dribbled the ball again, frowning at it.

"Look, it's the same ball we played with yesterday," Rain said. "But if you want your own ball, that's fine with us. We want you to have every advantage you can."

Masterson glared at Rain, then snorted. He went to the

top of the key and shot for outs. He drained the shot. He looked at Rain. "We don't need any advantages."

"You want ball or basket?" I said.

They could choose to have the ball first or they could choose which basket they wanted to shoot at. This was also part of my strategy. At this time of day, the sun shone at an angle so that on the near court, the sun would be in your eyes while shooting. But if you chose the far court, the sun would be in your eyes while defending your basket. I knew he would choose not to shoot into the sun, because that's what almost everyone picked. Most players focused on their shooting, because making baskets is what made them feel good.

However, because they had the height advantage, we knew they would be shooting most of their shots close to the basket, so the sun wouldn't be a major factor. But on defense, when we were snapping passes around, they'd be staring into the sun, giving us a fraction of a second to shoot before they got into defensive position.

"We'll take basket," Masterson said.

I grinned. I really was devious.

"We'll take that basket," he said, pointing to the one we didn't want him to take.

Uh-oh.

I looked at the rest of the team. Roger sighed heavily, as if we'd already lost. Gee shrugged as if he'd expected things to go wrong, as they always did when he had to go up against a bunch of rich Newport Beach kids. Tom showed no emotion. He just wanted to play, win or lose.

Rain laughed.

Then she ran around high-fiving us. "Yes!" she said.

Maybe she'd misunderstood the plan. Maybe she was going a little crazy.

"Ball," I said to Masterson. He passed it hard at my chest. I caught it without expression, as if a butterfly had just wandered into my hands, but the force had slightly jammed my index finger. The knuckle ached.

I stepped out-of-bounds next to the hoop pole to pass the ball in. Gee waited for the pass.

"Wrong side, loser," Masterson said, pointing to the other basket.

"Wait a minute," Roger said, "you chose this side."

"You can't do that!" Rain snapped. "You already picked!"

"I changed my mind, midget. Game hasn't started yet." Masterson grinned at her.

Rain slunk off down to the other side of the court. The rest of us looked as angry as possible as we glared at them on our way to the other side. As I got close to Rain, I whispered, "Well played, *midget*."

"A variation on the Sicilian Defense in chess," she said.

I just stared, not knowing what she was talking about.

"Reverse psychology," she explained.

"Oh," I said. "That's what I thought," I said.

We both laughed at that.

In pickup ball, the first few minutes of a game are the most important, because the teams don't know each other very well, so they're still feeling out the weaknesses and strengths. We'd played the Undertakers before, so we knew that they had a lot of strengths. But they also had the one weakness that sometimes allows the smaller team to pull an upset. Like the eighth-ranked Sixers defeating the Bulls in the 2012 play-offs. Or the 135th-ranked Steve Darcis defeating number one seed Rafael Nadal at Wimbledon in the first round in 2013.

Overconfidence.

Overconfidence makes players sloppy. They don't follow their shots as quickly, they're slower to jump into defense, they don't hustle down the court. I remembered what Brooke had said about fast versus slow zombies. Slow zombies made people overconfident and they ended up getting chomped on.

We had the pumped ball, we had the better court; now we needed to make them overconfident.

So we let them score the first five points. We pretended that we were trying our best, but we let ourselves get stopped by picks that we ordinarily would have fought through. We let ourselves get "surprised" by a pump-fake we ordinarily would have anticipated. It was a gamble, but we were desperate to even the odds. We sure weren't going to grow three inches and gain twenty pounds in the next few minutes, so we relied on our basic basketball skills— and my deviousness.

And it all worked as planned. Missed shots rebounded a little farther off the rim. We anticipated that and hung back from the hoop, giving us more second attempts and therefore more points. The sun messed with them on defense, so we passed the ball around a lot and shot from the spots where the sun was at our backs but directly in their eyes. That made them slower to get their hands up to block. Finally, giving them the first five points allowed them to relax a little, certain that they would crush us fast and be on their way home.

A fourth bonus was that Fauxhawk was so distracted checking his watch and searching the park for my brother that he didn't pay attention to the game. Why should he? There was no money riding on it. But that meant he didn't yell at his team, motivating them through fear.

When the score was 12–12, Fauxhawk called a time-out.

"Where the hell is your brother?" he hollered at me.

I checked my phone. I knew he wouldn't have texted or called, but I wanted to see how much of the fifteen minutes that he'd given me was left. Only eight minutes.

"Nothing new from him," I said. "But he told me he'd be here by the end of the game."

"I don't care about the stupid game!" Fauxhawk shouted. Then he slid closer to me and said, so that only I could hear him, "He'd better be here soon or I'm going to take it out on you, little brother. And I won't be as kind to you as I was to him. Ever try to shoot a basketball with a couple broken arms?"

"There's a lot of people around," I said.

He grinned. "Doesn't have to be here. Doesn't have to

be today. I'm a very patient man. One day you're riding your bike home and a van 'accidentally' clips you from behind. Instant tragedy."

I didn't say anything, just returned to the court to get the game rolling.

I tried not to think about his threat. I was counting on Jax. I was counting on being right about everything I'd figured out. That was a lot of counting.

A couple minutes later we had pulled ahead 17–14, and that's when the Undertakers got physical again. We knew they would, so we tried to avoid physical contact as much as possible. But in basketball, it's not always possible.

Masterson started it by charging through a pick that Tom had set for me. He rammed Tom so hard that Tom staggered into Rain, almost knocking her down.

"Offensive foul," I said, taking the ball to the top of the key.

"He was moving!" Masterson said.

"Seventeen to fourteen," I said, ignoring him. "Ball's in." I passed it in.

Danforth came down with a rebound, elbowing Roger on top of his head.

Clement straight-armed Gee in the chest in order to snag a loose ball.

Masterson pushed me toward the basket, using his butt. But I kept darting back and forth, swatting at the ball. I knocked it away once. He retrieved it, but he had to start pushing me all over again. I knew he was frustrated, and

I could tell by the tension in his body that he was about to do another shoulder fake, followed by a head smack in my face. Just as his head came backward, I ducked around his right side and stole the ball.

Masterson chased me downcourt like a hunting dog after a rabbit. But I was faster and managed a soft layup before he made it to the free throw line. I stopped and turned in time to see Masterson plow right into me, knocking me into the hoop pole. Fortunately, the pole had a thick green pad around it, but the impact knocked all the air out of me and I slumped to the ground, gasping.

My team ran over to help me up.

When Roger saw that I was okay and breathing normally, he spun with his fist up. "I'm gonna punch a hole in his face!"

I grabbed Roger's shoulder. "Let's just finish the game." I knew we were running out of time.

When I looked over at Masterson, I saw his team gathered around him arguing. Clearly, Lambert and Bendleton felt Masterson had gone too far. "Not cool, Phil," Lambert told Masterson. Bendleton nodded agreement. Masterson didn't seem to care, but I could see Danforth and Clement shift uncomfortably at the disagreement.

"Fine," Masterson said. "Let's just beat these little turds senseless and head down to Huntington Beach to check out the sand bunnies."

Disagreement over. They all liked that idea.

"Our ball," Masterson said, snapping his fingers at Rain, who'd snatched it up after my collision with the pole. She scowled fiercely at Masterson, gripping the ball as if she were about to hurl it into his face.

"C'mon, team," I said brightly to show I was okay, "let's finish this."

Both teams squared off to continue the game. Some of the Undertakers might have disagreed with cheap shots, but the determined looks on their faces showed that they still wanted to win.

My teammates also had the grim glares of warriors who want to win.

Nobody was giving an inch.

So, you probably want to know who won.

Did Good (us) defeat Evil (them)?

Did the Underdogs (us) beat the Top Dogs (them)?

Or was Coach right about the big guys almost always beating the smaller guys with the same skills?

But this isn't one of those slow-motion, final-shot-at-the-buzzer-to-win stories. We didn't try to make a philosophical or moral point. We didn't try to inspire anyone.

We just played basketball.

When it was over, nothing had changed. Masterson was still a jerk. Roger was still a hothead. We didn't hug, not even the customary hand slaps. The world wasn't a better, kinder, gentler place. No lessons were learned.

We just played basketball.

A bunch of kids being kids, playing a game that had no consequences for the future. It wouldn't be recorded anywhere.

Who won? What color is an orange? Who cares? We didn't play to entertain the spectators watching from the sidelines who shouted or clapped or winced at every play. We didn't even play for you, who are reading about the game. You know by now that I'm not one of those winning-doesn't-matter-it's-how-you-play-the-game guys. *I want to win*. But who won this particular game is a matter only for those who actually played it. Because we weren't thinking about any world except the world on that seventy-four-by-forty-two-foot greentop court. A constantly moving world in which everything was happening at once—and everything was at once both predictable and surprising.

We just played basketball.

And it was awesome.

Two minutes after the game was over, Jax arrived.

I was the only one not surprised by what happened next.

# WHO IS THE REAL CRIMINAL MASTERMIND?

**MOM** yanked open the door after the first knock. "I'm so sorry for the short notice, Hannah," she said anxiously. "Chris only just told us that he has an algebra test tomorrow." She lowered her voice, but I could still hear it from the kitchen. "I think he's starting to panic a little."

I was spying on them through the kitchen door.

Hannah smiled. "Not a problem, Mrs. Richards. But I only have half an hour before I have to meet another student. Why didn't he say something last night?"

Dad (worried): "He's been so distracted lately. He didn't even know about the test until he got home and opened his student planner. That really isn't like him."

Mom: "It's worth a fourth of his final grade."

Dad: "He begged us to call you. And he's not a kid who usually asks for help."

Hannah: "Then we'd better not waste a second. Kitchen?"

Mom: "Yes."

I tiptoed quickly back to my chair and sat. My algebra book was open and I pretended to be studying it.

The three of them came through the door, led by

Hannah. "Look at you, Chris, so studious," she said with a smile.

"I try," I said, smiling back.

That's when Jax came up behind Mom and Dad, draping his arms over their shoulders like the three of them were singing oldies songs at a party. "Hello, parental units," he said brightly. "Ready to be surprised?"

Oh, before we get to Jax's surprise, you probably want to know what went down at the park after Jax arrived. Here's what happened:

Jax strolled across the manicured grass carrying a cheap black backpack with some big-eyed Japanese anime boy on it. I guessed the stolen jewelry was inside.

As soon as Fauxhawk saw Jax, he ran over to meet him. At first he barked all kinds of curse words at Jax, asking him why he was late and so on. But he shut up when Jax handed him the backpack.

They were about twenty feet from the basketball court. Our game was over, so we all stood around, wiping sweat from our faces with the bottoms of our shirts, or drinking from our water bottles. I was the only one watching Jax and Fauxhawk, though I pretended not to be. I knew what was coming, so it was hard for me to act calm.

Fauxhawk unzipped the bag and rummaged inside without taking anything out. He bent down to study the contents more closely. Finally, he smiled wolfishly, slung the backpack over his shoulder, and shook Jax's hand.

"We're even," Fauxhawk said.

"Not quite," Jax said.

Fauxhawk looked confused for a second. During that moment, my brother grabbed Fauxhawk by the wrist, twisted it behind his back, forced him to the ground, knelt on his back with one knee, and slapped a pair of handcuffs onto his wrists. It all seemed to happen in one swift motion, like a perfectly executed pick-and-roll.

Fauxhawk's loud curses drew all our attention. A few parents at the playground grabbed their toddlers and carried them to their cars.

"What the—?" Roger said, his mouth hanging open in shock.

"Coach!" Masterson called, and he and the rest of the team started running toward Fauxhawk.

I didn't know what they were planning to do, so I started running, too.

It wasn't necessary. A bald guy in his twenties who'd been shooting free throws dropped his ball and ran toward my brother. As he moved, he pulled out a badge from his shorts and waved it. "Tustin PD!"

A bulky woman in a pink sweatsuit who'd been walking a black Lab also ran over, waving a badge and shouting, "Tustin PD!" The dog trotted obediently beside her.

When we all congregated around my brother; he was pulling Fauxhawk to his feet, saying, ". . . the right to an attorney. If you cannot afford one . . ."

He had his badge out, too. It was attached to a leather wallet, one flap of which was tucked into his shirt pocket so the shiny gold badge hung down in plain view. But it didn't look like the oval Tustin PD badges, which had a big gold scroll across the top that said POLICE OFFICER and in the middle two more scrolls that said TUSTIN POLICE.

Jax's badge was a seven-pointed star. In the middle was the image of a woman clutching a spear and wearing a gladiator helmet. The word EUREKA was embossed above her. Encircling that picture were the words CALIFORNIA HIGHWAY PATROL.

Roger, Rain, Tom, and Gee stood behind me watching.

Roger poked me hard in the back. "Dude, since when is your brother a cop?"

After Fauxhawk was driven off in a Tustin PD patrol car (was it one of the same ones we'd hidden under last night?), pick-up arrangements had to be made for the Gold Coasters. The woman cop with the dog drove Fauxhawk's van to the police station. Two uniformed officers awaited the arrival of the Gold Coasters' parents, who would probably be hysterical with worry.

Jax nodded for me to follow him to the parking lot. "I've got to head down to the station, bro, but I'll give you a ride home."

I said good-bye to my teammates and promised to fill them in tomorrow at school.

In the car I asked to see Jax's badge. He plucked it from his pocket and handed it to me. "This is cool," I said, rubbing my fingers across the surface.

"Each point on the star stands for something important

to being a Highway Patrol officer: Character, Integrity, Knowledge, Judgment, Honor, Loyalty, and Courtesy." He looked over at me. "You have any questions, Chris?"

"I thought the Highway Patrol just did traffic stuff. You know, like wrote speeding tickets on freeways and stuff. Stared at people behind those big hats and dark sunglasses."

"We do have awesome sunglasses."

"Can you get me a pair?"

He laughed. "I'll look into it."

"So what's the Highway Patrol doing taking down Fauxhawk?"

"Fauxhawk?"

"Rand."

"Nice," he said, chuckling. "The CHP has the power to enforce any state law anywhere in the state. Sometimes we help local cops with investigations by providing outside personnel for undercover work. Because I was familiar with the neighborhoods and the people, I was assigned to this case."

"As the loser who dropped out of Stanford? That was your cover?"

"Pretty much. I was supposed to have dropped out because I had a gambling problem."

"So you could make a big bet with Rand and deliberately lose."

"Yup. I needed to owe him enough money that once he accepted stolen goods as payment, we'd have a slam-dunk case on him."

"Yeah, but everything depended on us losing that first game. What would you have done if we'd have won?"

"You *did* have me worried," he said. "You've gotten a lot better since the last time I saw you."

"You looked pretty worried, but I thought it was because you were scared that we'd lose."

"My brilliant acting, bro," he said. "I'd done everything to stack it against you. I told you about the game late so it would be hard for you to get the best players. I didn't tell you that they were older and bigger, so you couldn't prepare. But you still almost took them down." He grinned proudly at me. "Anyway, if you'd have won, I would have just made another bet on something else. But that would have delayed the whole operation a few more days."

"A few more days of lying to Mom and Dad. And me."

Jax sighed heavily. "Yeah, about that. I'm sorry, man. I had to pretend to drink so Mom and Dad would react normally. This was my first undercover gig, Chris. I had to do it by the book. I wouldn't have done it this way if we'd had other options."

"You did have other options. You could have just told us the truth."

He gave me a skeptical look. "Really? You think Mom and Dad were ready to hear that I'd decided to ditch law school to become a cop?"

He had a good point. "But you could have told me," I said.

"If I'd told you, you would've had to keep it a secret

from Mom and Dad. You're not built that way, bro. Look how much keeping your comic book stuff from them is eating you up."

I didn't say anything to that. I had to think about it.

"Anyway, the thing is, we knew from CIs that—"

"CIs?"

"Confidential informants. Snitches."

"Right."

Jax continued: "We knew that Rand had received the stolen goods from those garage burglaries and was selling them. But we didn't have enough proof. Now we do."

I thought about that for a moment, then said, "So our burglary last night wasn't just about getting the stolen goods, because you could have gotten them from your own department."

"We had to make sure Rand thought the stolen jewelry was really stolen."

"That's why you deliberately triggered the alarm. You wanted it to be in the newspapers and on the news so Rand would know about it. You wanted the cops to have your photo so Rand would know it was you."

"You caught that, huh? Very good."

"I've seen you dribble through an entire team's defense. I've seen you toss a touchdown pass a split second before getting mauled by three offensive players. You don't rattle and you don't trip."

"I *am* good, aren't I?"

"Not that good, or I wouldn't have figured it out."

He laughed. "Touché, SP."

"Were the local cops in on it when they showed up at Angelo's last night?"

He looked over at me, surprised. "Of course. Do you think there's any way I'd put you in any real danger? Even Angelo helped us with the sting."

I sighed with disappointment. "So my debut as Master Thief was just smoke and mirrors."

"Not at all. It was important that the heist looked authentic and not staged. Your breaking through the carpet store's wall and using the vacuum cleaner was great. When Rand heard about it, he thought I was some sort of criminal genius. Wanted me to do some more heists for him."

"What about Officer Crane at school?"

"Yeah, I told him to go at you hard. I wanted the rumor that I was involved to get started there. That way, if Rand checked, he would have more confirmation that I robbed the place." He paused to give me a stern look. "I also wanted him to scare you a little, to let you know that breaking into places isn't a game. It has real consequences. And those consequences aren't fun."

I was about to protest that I wasn't an idiot, when suddenly my phone buzzed. It was a text from Theo with the information I'd asked for. I smiled. Now I knew the final piece of the puzzle.

# THE CONFESSIONS OF JAX RICHARDS, UNDERCOVER COP

**JAX** reached over and mussed my hair. "I have to admit, you scared the crap out of me when you sent that text. 'I know everything.' Pretty melodramatic, dude."

"Got your attention."

"Yeah, speaking of that. How'd you figure it all out? I know you didn't call the CHP, because they would have denied I worked for them."

"No, I didn't know anything for sure. I just had suspicions. I guess in the end it was more about who you are, Jax. The whole dropping out of Stanford Law School didn't make sense. You've never quit anything. That's not you. Neither is the gambling or the drinking or deliberately making Mom and Dad miserable. Not to mention lying to me."

He frowned and shook his head sadly. "Sorry about that, Chris. That was the hardest part."

"After I found out you'd never attended Stanford Law—"

"Yeah, about that. How'd you find out? The CHP went through a lot of trouble to build that alibi in case Rand checked me out."

I told him about Theo's calls to the university.

Jax laughed. "I'll pass that along to my boss so they do a better job next time. Thank goodness Rand isn't as smart as you and Theo. Go on."

"So, after I realized you'd never been to Stanford, I wondered what you might have done during that time instead. Dad told me how much you hated injustice as a kid. 'You're out of order! You're out of order! The whole trial is out of order!' Remember that?"

"Yeah, of course. Al Pacino yelling at the judge and getting hauled off to jail for contempt. Classic scene."

"I knew you'd still feel that way. You couldn't have changed that much. So, I started looking at the little things. You're in better physical shape than ever. That doesn't go with being a heavy-drinking dropout with a gambling problem. But it does go with being a cop."

He made a face. "Weak."

"Agreed. But once I realized you wanted us to lose that game against the Undertakers, it raised a whole new set of questions. And the answers kept coming back to you still being a good guy pretending to be bad. Like a secret identity."

"A little better," he said.

"Finally, I knew you'd deliberately set off that alarm in

the pawnshop. When I asked myself why you'd do that, everything fell into place. You were setting a trap."

He thought about that, then said, "But you agreed to help me before the alarm, SP. How does your logic account for that?"

"It doesn't. Except I knew you'd never put me in jeopardy unless you had a Get Out of Jail Free card. Never."

"So it was pretty much blind faith."

"Not blind. But faith in you. The Jax I knew."

He looked straight ahead for a minute and I could see that he was choked up. Tears brimmed in his eyes.

I punched his shoulder. "Don't get sentimental on me, copper."

He chuckled.

"Anyway, you still don't have the mastermind behind the garage burglaries and you don't know how they're doing it."

Jax shrugged. "We'll sweat it out of Rand. He's not exactly a supervillain. Real bad guys usually can't wait to rat out someone if it'll help their own case."

"I don't think he'll rat," I said.

"Really, Batman? And why is that?"

"Because it's not just about money. He has another motive."

"What do you mean?"

I told him what I meant.

"Holy crap!" he said. "Maybe I acted too quickly."

"Don't worry," I said. I told him my plan.

"Holy crap!" he said again.

I said, "The CHP really teaches you how to express yourself eloquently."

He punched me in the shoulder. Hard. "How's that for eloquent?"

I rubbed my shoulder. "I have another question."

"Yeah?"

"How are you going to sedate Mom and Dad so you can tell them the truth?"

# MOM AND DAD ARE GONNA FAINT

**BACK** to the kitchen:

"Miss me?" Jax said, kissing Mom loudly on the cheek. "You're not getting out of this, Pop," he said, and then kissed Dad on the cheek.

Despite their disappointment in what they thought was Jax throwing away his law career, they still couldn't help but show their love for him under his playful embrace. Mom actually giggled.

"We'd better let them get to it," Dad said, finding his Dad Voice. "Chris has a big test tomorrow and Hannah can only stay half an hour."

"Ah yes, my almost prom date," Jax said, smiling at Hannah.

"Jax," Hannah said coldly.

"Hannah," Jax said, mocking her serious tone.

Hannah looked at my parents for help. "We have twenty-five minutes left."

Mom started to push Jax out of the kitchen. "Let's leave them alone," she said.

"Actually," Jax said, "we'll only need five minutes." He pulled out a pair of handcuffs from his back pocket and dangled them in front of Hannah. "You're under arrest, Hannah Selby." He informed her of the charges and her rights as he cuffed her arms behind her back.

"I want to call my attorney," she said.

"As soon as you get to the station," Jax said, and he led her outside to the two cops waiting for her.

I didn't pay attention to any of that. I was busy watching the wide-eyed expressions on Mom's and Dad's faces. They muttered a few sentences ("What are you doing, Jax?" "This isn't funny, son!" "Hannah, what's he talking about?"—stuff like that). But they ran out of steam pretty quickly. They looked pale and breathless, as if they were about to faint, so I held out chairs for both of them at the kitchen table.

They sat quietly for a moment, catching their breath and adjusting to the new reality.

"Do you know what's going on, Chris?" Mom asked, the first to return to lawyer mode. Her voice was calm and steady.

"Let's wait for Jax," I said.

"Son," Dad said sharply, "tell us what's going on right now!"

"He'll be back in a minute," I said, holding firm.

They seemed too tired or stunned to fight me, so we just waited in silence.

A couple minutes later, Jax walked in and clapped cheerfully like a game-show host trying to pump up the audience. "All righty! Bet you have some questions?"

Actually, all things considered, what followed was pretty civil. Jax explained that he'd decided after graduating from college that law school wasn't for him. He didn't want to sit at a desk researching law cases, making backroom deals, working on cases that could drag on for months or even years. He wanted to catch bad guys and make the world safer right now.

"Why didn't you just tell us that?" Mom said, a crack in her voice.

"Because you would have tried to talk me out of it. You would have presented a logical case with brilliant arguments. You would have told me that there were lots of good men and women who felt the way I did and who would make fine police officers. Then you'd point out that there were not many who had my test scores and grades and who would make first-rate lawyers. You would have told me that the work is dangerous and I might get killed. You would have reminded me of what that would do to the family. All of which is true. And I couldn't take the chance of you talking me out of it."

Mom and Dad swore that they would have been understanding. And I know they like to think of themselves as the kind of people who would have been understanding. But I don't think they would have been. They were still the same nervous parents who stood in the pool and watched their toddler son (me) swim the four feet from one to the other, the water around them practically boiling from their anxiety.

Jax told them about his undercover assignment and how he had to pretend to be a drinking, gambling idiot. And how it had led to the arrest of a serious criminal. He'd left out the part about us robbing the pawnshop, his beating, and how he'd used me and my friends to lose the money.

That was a good call by him. Otherwise, we'd be using live electrical wires we'd yanked from a lamp cord to restart their hearts.

Eventually, the conversation got around to Hannah. Jax explained to them that she was the mastermind behind the garage burglaries.

Dad looked like Jax had karate-chopped him in the throat. Mom looked like she felt a tarantula crawling up her leg under her pants.

"Actually," Jax said, "it was Chris who figured out that part. So, I'll let him explain."

# MY BRILLIANT CHECKLIST OF CLUES

**HERE'S** basically what I told them:

**Clue No. 1:** Hannah had told Jax that she had attended the University of Arizona in Phoenix. Today, Fauxhawk/ Rand was wearing a hoodie with a white *A* that is the symbol of the University of Arizona. Fauxhawk also said he'd played on a team called the Wildcats, which is the name of the U of A team. (Remember Jax saying, "Go, Wildcats!" to Hannah the first time she was at our house?) They are about the same age, so that could put them at the U of A in Phoenix at the same time.
**Clue Grade:** B–. Interesting, but not conclusive. After all, there are twenty-seven colleges with teams called the Wildcats. (I looked it up.)

"How did you know the *A* on his hoodie was from the University of Arizona?" Mom asked.

"I saw their basketball team play during March Madness. Remember, Dad?"

Dad nodded and said to Mom, "We did." Then he gave

me a little smile, like he was impressed. "How did you remember that?"

I shrugged. I didn't know why I remembered the stuff I did (and forgot stuff about math equations and periodic charts right before a test). Somehow, when I thought back on the last few days, little inconsistencies floated in my mind like dead flies in a bowl of milk. And I would think about them until I figured out what was wrong.

**Clue No. 2:** Last night after tutoring, Hannah had nodded at my bruised face and said, "The Jax I knew in high school wouldn't have let that happen." At the time, I was touched by her concern. But later I remembered that I'd never told her that Jax was at the game. The only way she would have known is if Fauxhawk or one of the Undertakers had told her. She'd also said that the other team had disrespected me in "my house." How did she know we'd played at the park? That made me think back to that first night, when she'd asked when Mom and Dad would be home from work, and when I'd be home from school. It was more like she wanted to know when the house would be empty.

**Clue Grade:** A–. Together with Clue No. 1, pretty solid.

Mom and Dad exchanged looks. Silent parental communication passed between them, like insects. Then Mom turned to Jax and scolded, "You bet on his game? Didn't you think that betting might lead them to become more violent?"

Oops. I forgot that we hadn't told them that part. Jax gave me a thanks-a-lot glare.

Dad laid a hand on Mom's arm. "It's done, sweetheart." What he meant was: *This kind of reaction is why Jax didn't tell us anything in the first place.* Mom nodded. What she meant was: *We'll wait until later before tearing into both of them.*

Silent communication is pretty cool. I had the silent part down; now I needed to learn how to use it to actually tell people stuff. I guess it's a parent-to-parent thing.

"Okay," Mom said. Then she looked at me. "Not bad reasoning, Chris."

"But it wouldn't hold up in court," Dad pointed out. "She could claim that you said it during your tutoring session. Or that she overheard it from another student she tutored. Classic case of he said/she said."

Mom smiled at me. "Still, not bad."

"There's more," I said, encouraged.

**Clue No. 3:** I'd asked Theo to find out the ages of the children in the homes that had been burglarized, because whenever someone mentioned stolen goods, they listed kids' bicycles. Theo found out that each of the families had a child under ten. What's one of the things young children have in common? *Babysitters.*

Where do babysitters come from? High school, mostly. Theo called the burglary victims to ask if they could recommend any babysitters. After that he called the babysitters' parents to ask if they could recommend any tutors. He got enough information to draw links between the burglary victims, the babysitters they used, and the person who tutored the babysitters: Hannah.
**Clue Grade:** A+.

Mom thought about that. "Wait a minute. So the baby-sitters pulled the burglaries? I thought the robberies took place when no one was home."

"They didn't commit the actual robberies themselves. They just made it possible for the real burglars to gain entry."

"How?" Mom asked. "Did they steal keys?"

"No, that would've been too risky. They did something much more clever."

I paused here for dramatic effect. I didn't get many opportunities in a house full of really smart people to have my own "genius moment." I was definitely going to make it last.

"Are we going to have to wait for the movie to find out?" Mom said.

"They didn't need a key," I said. "What they did do was steal the remote code to the garage door openers . . ."

[This next part is where I explained how they got those codes and used them to break in, which I'm sure as heck not going to tell you guys, because I don't want you thinking, Hey, that would be fun, and getting arrested. Leave the Master Thief stuff to us professionals.]

". . . and once Hannah had the code, she'd give it to Fauxhawk, and he'd program a new remote device to open the door when no one was home. He'd drive over in his van with the pool services sign on the side, and no one would suspect anything."

"Babysitters," Mom said, shaking her head. "Remember when I used to read those Baby-sitters Club books to you when you were little?"

"No," I said. Of course, I did remember, but I wanted to stop Mom from ever bringing it up again, especially in front of my friends.

"This was the Evil Baby-sitters Club," Jax said.

"But why would these babysitters do it?" Dad asked. "It's not like we live in a bad neighborhood. These kids all come from good homes."

"Crime isn't always about background, Dad," Jax said. "Hannah tutored dozens of kids, so she had a lot to choose from. She only needed a few bad apples. Those who were babysitting obviously needed money, so she picked kids who seemed especially troubled. She'd pay each a few hundred bucks to do something with very little risk. Thousands of kids shoplift every day. They take a much greater risk for a lot less reward."

I didn't say anything. My shoplifting adventure would stay between me and Brooke.

"But they're kids," Dad said, getting a little angry at the idea of someone using children to commit crimes.

"Exactly," I said. "Easy for someone smart, like Hannah, to manipulate. And kids never think they'll get caught." Something I knew from experience.

"But how could Hannah be sure they wouldn't tell their friends, or get a bad case of the guilts and confess to their parents?" Dad asked.

"Guess she figured they didn't want to go to jail any more than she did."

"I get why kids might do it. Extra money. Maybe even the thrill of doing something unlawful," Mom said. "But I don't understand why Hannah would. She is pretty, smart, has—had—a good tutoring business . . . her master's degree." She made a face as if the idea was too bitter to hold in her head.

"She did it for the money, Mom," Jax said. "Just like every other crook, from convenience-store robber to the white-collar billionaire. Tustin PD estimated they stole more than a hundred thousand dollars' worth of goods. That's a lot of tutoring hours."

"I think she did it because she was Rand's girlfriend," I said. "They met in college, and when he started being a criminal, she helped him. Like a family business or something."

"Such a waste," Mom said.

I shrugged. I didn't feel sorry for Hannah. She chose to help rob those families. She'd gone through all that education and came out with the conclusion that she deserved what others had by stealing it. Then I thought, Isn't that what Master Thief thinks?

I shook my head, not wanting to think about that right now.

"You know, Chris," Mom said, "I'm very impressed by your reasoning. Well done, son."

"Well done?" Dad jumped out of his chair. "It's better than well done. What my son did was nothing short of terrific! I can't believe you put all that together yourself. You have the first-rate analytical mind of a lawyer, Chris."

*Not of a lawyer*, I wanted to say, *but of a writer. A comic book writer.* But I said nothing.

"I say we all go out to dinner," Dad said. "All this 'well done' talk has made me hungry for steak. Jax, you can fill us in on what you've been doing at the CHP."

"Sorry, Dad. I have to go down to the station," Jax said. "And our boy genius has other plans, too. He has to be somewhere by six."

"Where?" Dad asked. "It's a school night."

"A girl's house. She invited him." He grinned at me, and I know it took every bit of his strength not to tease me.

Mom and Dad exchanged looks again. This one said: *He's never been to a girl's house. What are they going to do together? Should we have The Talk with him? Should we let him go?*

"Her name is Brooke Hill. We're just going to watch some French movie that Mr. Laubaugh gave her."

Another exchange of concerned looks: *French? Sounds dirty.*

"What's the film?" Dad asked. He liked to think of himself as a foreign-movie expert.

*"The 400 Blows."*

His face lit up. "Oh, that's excellent. French New Wave, directed by François Truffaut. He's one of my favorites. Remember *Day for Night*, Denise? Let's see, what else has he directed?"

He was determined to ruin it by Wikipedia-ing all over the place.

"Are her parents going to be home?" Mom asked, thankfully cutting Dad off.

"Yes." I was guessing on this one.

"I'll make sure when I drop him off," Jax volunteered. "No parents, no movie, Mister Smooth."

It was weird, but now that all the mysteries were solved, I no longer cared about basking in the glory of victory. I didn't care about Fauxhawk or Hannah or the Undertakers. I just wanted to see Brooke.

I stared at Mom and Dad, waiting for their answer. *Could I go to a girl's house to watch a French film?* The pool water boiled around them.

# THE TALKING CURE

**"WOW!"** Jax said when we pulled up to the giant iron gate. "This place looks like it could withstand a Viking attack." Huge stone walls extended from the gate. On top of the walls were two feet of razor wire. "All it needs now is a shark-filled moat."

He pressed a button on the speaker box. "Hello?"

Brooke's voice crackled through the intercom, "Right on time. Come on up."

The intercom buzzed off. The iron gate slowly opened, the way creaky doors open in horror films.

"She didn't even ask who it was," Jax said. "Trusting."

"Not really," I said, pointing at the video cameras hidden in the bushes and aimed at us.

"Master Thief strikes again," he said.

We drove through and started up a long winding road. It took another few minutes through some woods before we arrived in a circular driveway so large that it could have hosted the Super Bowl.

"I hate to repeat myself," Jax said, "but wowwww!"

The house looked like an English castle, constructed

by stacking giant blocks of stone on top of each other. We got out of the car and walked to the front door, which was made of black wood and was the size of a garage door. Knocking on it made me feel like I might wake a dragon.

Fortunately, we didn't have to wait long. Brooke pulled it open and said, "Welcome."

I just stared at her. If I'd seen her on the street, I might not have recognized her.

Jax tried to bail me out with, "Hi, I'm Jax, Chris's handsomer brother. Lovely home."

"Be it ever so humble," she said. "I'm Brooke." They shook hands.

"You look different," I said, finally finding my voice.

"I have no idea how to take that," Brooke said. "Different like hideous monster under the bed? Or different like brilliant but approachable goddess?"

I meant that at school she wore the fanciest clothes. Everything she wore kind of glittered or shimmered or glowed. There were other girls at school whose parents dressed them in expensive clothing from exclusive shops, but somehow Brooke carried it off better. I think it's because you could tell she didn't really care about the clothes or the shoes or the jewelry. They were more like a costume to her.

Standing in front of me now, she wore white denim shorts that went to her knees, a loose blue sweatshirt with a red moose on it, and a pair of black-rimmed glasses. She was barefoot, with a thin silver ring around her pinkie toe.

"I just didn't know you wore glasses," I said, trying to recover.

"Smooth," she said, and Jax laughed. "I wear them for watching TV. Contacts irritate my eyes."

"Oh," I said. Then added, "They look good on you."

"Of course they do," she said. "Why wouldn't they?"

"Where are your parents?" Jax asked. "Not prying, just following parental orders."

"Downstairs in the basement, scrubbing the meth lab," she said.

Jax laughed again and nudged me. "This is going to be an interesting night, bro."

Brooke pointed at two sets of marble stairways that curved up to the second floor. "Mom's upstairs. She'll be down in a minute, so you don't have to worry. No hanky-panky or whatever you oldsters call it."

"Oldster?!" Jax said in mock offense. "I'm only twenty-two."

"Wow. You're even older than I thought."

Jax threw up his hands in surrender. "Okay, you win. Oldster it is."

Brooke laughed. They were getting along so well I was starting to wish he'd leave. Jax must have seen that on my face because he suddenly said, "I've gotta book, kids. Be back at nine sharp." He shook a warning finger at Brooke. "I want him in one piece, Dragon Lady."

She shrugged. "We'll see."

Jax left, winking at me as he did.

Dude, who winks anymore?

"Follow me," Brooke said. She took me through rooms so lavish they might have been in a movie about rich people forced to spend as much money as possible every day. Through the windows that looked out on the backyard, I saw a swimming pool the size of a lake, with three waterfalls of different heights. Several automatic pool cleaners floated on top, sucking up dead bugs and leaves.

Finally, we came to a room that had an actual movie marquee over the door. The black letters spelled out: WELCOME CHRIS.

"I know there should be a comma before your name, but I couldn't find one."

"I won't report you to the punctuation police this one time."

We entered the room, which was a tiny movie theater with about twenty actual movie seats. Except these were leather and they flipped back like my dad's La-Z-Boy chair. Each had a wooden cup holder. In the back corner sat a small popcorn machine and a soda fountain with Coke, Diet Coke, root beer, and lemonade.

"Help yourself," Brooke said. "I'll be right back. I have to go get that surprise I told you about."

"Can I get you a drink or something?" I asked.

"Yeah, thanks. A lemonade and a bag of popcorn."

I got the drinks and a couple popcorns and sat in the front seat. The screen was the size of my bedroom wall.

I wasn't sure how I felt right then. Nervous. Excited.

Scared. I just wished she'd get back and start the movie so I could sit in the dark with my thoughts.

After a couple minutes of drinking my Coke and eating popcorn, I heard the door open behind me. "You are so lucky!" I said. "This is the coolest theater ever."

"You're right, Chris," the woman's voice said. "I am lucky."

I turned in my leather chair and saw a woman who looked like an older version of Brooke. Except this woman was hunched over, supporting herself on two metal forearm crutches. She started walking slowly forward, and I could see by the tightness in her face that each step caused her pain.

I jumped up and walked quickly to her so she wouldn't have to move. "Hi, I'm Chris Richards." I didn't know if I should offer to shake hands. Would she lose her balance and fall if she tried?

She raised her right hand for me to shake. I did, and felt a slight trembling in her fingers as we shook.

"I'm Ellie, Brooke's mom. You're the first friend she's had to the house in three years, so I just had to come see you for myself."

I didn't know what to say to that. I couldn't help but feel like I would disappoint her. She didn't seem disappointed. She smiled brightly. Then she slowly turned and started back out the door. "I hope you two have a lovely evening. The film is one of my favorites."

Had everybody but us heard of this dumb French film?

"Can I help you . . . ?" I asked, though I wasn't sure what I could help her with. I just didn't like standing by helplessly while she staggered up the aisle.

She laughed sweetly in a way that reminded me of my mom. "No, Chris, I'm used to this now. I have an elevator that will take me back to my room. But I have hidden cameras in this room, so if you try anything with my daughter, you'll be surprised at just how fast I can move." She whacked the side of a seat with her crutch.

"Oh, I . . . I won't try anything."

She laughed again. "I'm just kidding, Chris. There are no cameras. But if there were, they'd be for *your* protection, not Brooke's."

She chuckled as she worked her way out the door.

"Nice meeting you," I called after her.

Outside the door, I heard Brooke and her mom talking, though I couldn't make out the words. Then they both laughed in a way that sounded like they were harmonizing. It made me smile to hear it.

Brooke entered the room with a red folder. I reached for it, but she pulled it back. "Later," she said in a way that said there would be no arguing.

We sat in our seats and she picked up the remote. "Parkinson's," she said to me. "That's what she has. In case you were wondering."

"I've heard of that. It's what Muhammad Ali has. And Olympic cyclist Davis Phinney."

"And Michael J. Fox."

I shook my head, not recognizing the name.

"He's an actor," she said. "He was in those *Back to the Future* movies."

"Oh, right. I've seen those. He also starred in that old movie *Teen Wolf* where he becomes a werewolf and plays great basketball."

"That's him. Anyway, it's a degenerative disorder of the central nervous system. Causes shaking, rigid movements, slowness, trouble with walking."

"Is there a cure?"

Brooke shook her head. "Nope. She's just going to keep getting worse."

I didn't know the right thing to say. I remembered that discussion in Mr. Laubaugh's class about the poem "Do Not Go Gentle into That Good Night." And how she'd been so detached when talking about death. Maybe because she'd been living with her mom's illness for so long.

I didn't want to make her sad, but I didn't want to pretend nothing had happened. I had to say something.

"Is that why you never invite anyone to your house?" I asked. "Are you afraid kids will make fun of you?"

She shook her head. "Just the opposite. I'm afraid they'll get all weepy and sympathetic and I'll have to put up with their sad doe eyes and constantly asking me, 'How are you today, Brooke?' or 'Is there anything we can do to help, Brooke?' Then everyone will be quick to cut me slack or forgive me for anything I do. Then where am I? Who am I? I'll be the kid who has an excuse to fail." She shook her head as if she was having a heated conversation with herself. "Let's just watch the movie."

She pressed the remote, and the lights went down. She pressed another button, and the DVD started.

The screen filled with a black-and-white image of an empty Paris street. I knew it was Paris because the Eiffel Tower was in the background. The name *Jean-Pierre Léaud* appeared, and under that was the word *dans*. I figured that must be the star. Then the words *Les Quatre Cents Coups* appeared. *Quatre* sounded like *cuatro* in Spanish, which meant four. *Cents* was like century, which meant hundred. *The 400 Blows*.

I looked over at Brooke, but she just stared straight ahead at the screen. Light and shadow flickered across her face like a flock of birds. I didn't want to seem creepy, so I, too, turned to the screen, glancing at her out of the corner of my eye. I knew she was probably doing the same thing. Neither of us wanted to be caught looking at the other.

That's when I realized something about her—I guess about both of us. We were both prisoners in a way, like the boy on the DVD cover looking through the fence. I was a prisoner of my own silence, keeping quiet so people could see me as they wanted to see me. But Brooke was a prisoner of her voice, of talking and snorting and attitude, so people would see her the way she demanded that they see her. Yet, neither of those versions was the real us. To see the real us, you had to look out of the corner of your eyes.

I don't know if I was right or not, but just thinking

about it made me feel better. I offered her some of my pop-corn, even though she had a full bag in her cup holder. She looked over at me, smiled, and reached into my bag. She tried to take so much popcorn in one grasp that her hand ripped the bag and popcorn spilled out on both of us.

We both laughed and sat back to enjoy the movie.

Actually, the movie was pretty good, despite all the French, and the small subtitles, and it being in black and white. I could see what my dad, Mr. Laubaugh, and Brooke's mom liked about it.

Then suddenly, about an hour in, the movie stopped and the lights came on.

I looked around in a panic, afraid I'd see Brooke's mom glaring down at both of us, even though we hadn't done anything.

But then I saw the remote in Brooke's hand.

"I couldn't wait any longer," she said excitedly. She opened the red folder she'd brought from her room and handed me a sheet of drawing paper.

I opened it. As I stared at the paper, my heart gave an extra thunk.

On the sheet was a beautifully drawn black ink figure of a man in his twenties leaning against a doorjamb. He was dressed elegantly in an expensive suit, yet he wore it in a way that made it look casual. Sunglasses were slid halfway down his nose, so you could see the roguish twin-kle in his eye. His slight grin announced to the world that he was afraid of nothing except being bored by too few dangerous challenges. When you looked closer, you could see through the door behind him the faint outline of the *Mona Lisa* on the wall. He was in the Louvre Museum, preparing to steal.

Beneath the drawing in bold lettering: *Master Thief.*

"This is amazing, Brooke. You didn't tell me you could draw."

"I can draw," she said.

"It's so professional. This could be in an actual comic book. It's that good." I couldn't stop myself from gushing. It was the first time I'd actually seen Master Thief as I had imagined him.

"I have one even better," she said. "I did it after talking to Theo. He told me you were working on solving the garage burglaries."

"You asked him about me?"

"I asked him why a cop had pulled you into the principal's office. That's when he told me the cops wanted your help."

Good ol' Theo.

I shrugged. "A little."

She handed me another sheet of drawing paper.

I stopped breathing.

This was no roguish thief in a shiny suit, driving a Ferrari and living in fancy hotels. It was a boy wearing jeans and a flannel shirt over a T-shirt. He had a backpack slung over one shoulder and a basketball under his other arm. And he had my face. Except it was my face smiling and confident and open. No secrets. It was me the way I wanted to be. Only I hadn't even known that until just now.

Beneath the drawing in bold lettering: *Master Sleuth*.

"Maybe you've been having trouble with your story because you're telling the wrong story," she said.

"What are his superpowers?" I asked.

"Doesn't have any," she said. "Doesn't need any."

I started breathing again. Brooke had drawn this picture before I'd actually solved the case. She saw it in me before I did.

You probably want to know what happened next. Just like you wanted to know who won the rematch between us and the Undertakers. This time I'll tell you some of what happened.

We talked.

I told her about what had happened with Jax and Fauxhawk and Hannah. I told her about me being a designer baby. I told her everything I could think of.

We never got around to watching the rest of the movie.

We just talked.

And it was awesome.

*What color is an orange?*

Any color it wants to be.

If you liked this book, look for

# SASQUATCH IN THE PAINT
## STREETBALL CREW BOOK ONE

by Kareem Abdul-Jabbar and Raymond Obstfeld

★"A crisp tale of sports, smarts and what it means to be your own man. . . . [T]his obviously is a work of someone intimate with sports and, by extension, how sports can serve as metaphor for a way of being in the world."
—*Kirkus Reviews* (starred review)

"This funny and inspirational story based on Kareem's sudden growth spurt as a middle-schooler captures the excitement of playing basketball and the anxiety of growing up—while growing tall, which I know a little something about. Kids will learn about the wonderful world of basketball and the importance of friendship and following your dreams." —Magic Johnson

"The pages fly. It has a great message."—Dr. Phil McGraw

"This smart, sensitive novel is full of simple truths that extend far beyond the court." —*Booklist*

"[A] humorous novel that delivers a heartwarming story about growing up, facing down bullies, and learning what true friendship is all about." —*School Library Journal*

"The depth and realism Abdul-Jabbar and Obstfeld bring to the novel keep it from being a run-of-the-mill sports story. . . . Readers will feel a kinship with Theo as he maneuvers through tough but realistic choices."

—*Publishers Weekly*

"*Sasquatch in the Paint* is terrific. . . . Here's how you know you're reading a really good book: when you get to the last page, but keep turning, looking for more. Honestly— that's what I did."

—Barry Saunders, *Raleigh News and Observer*

A Junior Library Guild Selection